I0682180

UFOs Confidential!
THE MEANING BEHIND THE
MOST CLOSELY GUARDED
SECRET OF ALL TIME
By
George Hunt Williamson
&
John McCoy

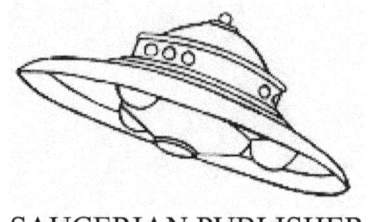

SAUCERIAN PUBLISHER
Original Sources in Ufology

Copyright © 2024, Saucerian Publisher

All rights reserve

9 781955 087636

ISBN: 978-1-955087-63-6

Al rights reserved. No part of this publication maybe reproduced, translate, store in a retrieval system, or transmitted in any form or by any means, electronic, mechanical, photocopying, recording or otherwise, without prior written permission from the publisher.

CONTENTS

UFOs CONFIDENTIAL!

STATE OF ARIZONA)
) ss.   AFFIDAVIT

County of Navajo)

    We the undersigned, being first duly sworn do solemnly swear; that the Documentary
Report of Interstellar Communication by Radiotelegraphy entitled: "THE SAUCERS
SPEAK", is accurate and true. We have been witnesses to and participants in these
happenings as listed in the above report. We also state that we are trained
observers by the very nature of our various occupations. We agree that a fact is
not a fact until it is proven; and that much time, effort and research has gone into
the above report to prove beyond any doubt its statements to be absolute fact. Our
work was carried on in the acceptable and standard form of scientific research employed by radio operators, anthropologists, and others. We also state that many
tests were performed under exacting conditions.

    We are thoroughly convinced that the "Flying Saucer" phenomena is interplanetary
in origin; that the mission of these ships to our Earth is a friendly one; that the
"saucer" intelligences have developed ESP (Extra-Sensory Perception) to a high degree;
and that these intelligences are of the human race inhabiting other heavenly bodies
and are now attempting contact with any inhabitants of the planet Earth who are
receptive to the Universal Truth.

    We also swear that we are not members of any organization (religious, scientific,
etc.) that would in any way profit or gain from our research. We are not propagating
a dogma or creed and none of us involved would gain by perpetrating a hoax.

    This report is being given to the people of the world because the facts contained
therein were not given to us for our own elucidation, but are for all those seeking
and desiring Universal Truth.

    That the undersigned Lyman N. Streeter, on oath deposes; that he received the
messages in International Morse Code.

Lyman H. Streeter, Jr.
Winslow, Arizona
Licensed Radio Operator, W7OJQ

Susan Streeter
Winslow, Arizona
Housewife

George H. Williamson, Sc.D.
Prescott, Arizona
Anthropologist

Betty Bowen
Winslow, Arizona
Student

Betty J. Williamson, B.S. A. B.
Prescott, Arizona
Chemist and Anthropologist

Ronald Tucker
Winslow, Arizona
Student

Alfred C. Bailey
Winslow, Arizona
Conductor, Santa Fe Railroad

Betty M. Bailey
Winslow, Arizona
Housewife

Subscribed and sworn to before me this 7th day of March, 1953.

Notary Public
Winslow, Arizona

My Commission Expires 10/26/56

1

FOREWORD

You are about to read a book that thousands said could never be written. Yet, it had to be written! In the first part you will find the causes behind the most closely guarded secret of all time. You will learn about the "curtain" that dropped over sixteen radio operators after they had successfully communicated with intelligences in outer space. You will be shocked and amazed when you realize that there is a "Hidden Empire" working secretly in the world and plotting its downfall. Many of the enigmatic problems of space visitation will suddenly take on a stark reality from the background you are about to receive. Why have other living beings come millions of miles through interstellar space to survey and study the Earth? The answer is in this book.

In the second part you will travel with the authors on a 30,000-mile journey through all parts of the United States and Canada . . . here you will find the effects created by the happenings discussed in Part One. You will realize that a startling pattern is now emerging . . . a Divine Plan that is guiding all men on Earth to join the "sheep" or the "goats" as the Father's "Flock" gathers together. This is the moment of decision for Earth . . . read this book and make yours! The material presented here is definitely not for the uninitiated . . . it is, as the title implies: UFOs CONFIDENTIAL!

THE AUTHORS

PART I (George Hunt Williamson)

RADIO CONTACT WITH OUTER SPACE

This first section of UFOs Confidential is dedicated to the memory of the young radioman, who in 1952 made contact with intelligences from outer space via radio-telegraphy and radiotelephony. Not wishing to disclose his identity in the book, THE SAUCERS SPEAK! I called him simply: Mr. "R" (for radio.") In the years ahead of us, when history speaks of the turbulent Twentieth Century on Earth, and when all war, disease, greed and selfishness have become nebulous things of ancient legend, Mr. 'R" will be remembered as a pioneer of the days when Earthman learned that he was not alone in the Universe.

Mr. "R" was the first radio operator to become a chan-nel between the small planet we call home and the vast-ness of interstellar space. He became a "bridge" for men of goodwill throughout the Father's limitless realm.

Now his key is silent . . . for he has graduated to an-other dimension of time and space . . . he is now free of the restrictions of Earth . . . free to communicate forever with worlds without number.

We say, "Goodbye," for just a little while, Mr. "R" . . . Light . . . Love . . . Peace . . . as you travel the Great Path up to the stars!

After the highly successful radio experiments of 1952-53, our group decided to write a book on our experiences. We realized that the information we had received was of the greatest importance to all mankind. We asked Mr. "R" if he cared to write a book about his radio contacts with outer space, and he said that he was not interested in making his experiments known publicly, but he didn't care if others wrote about them. At that time we had him sign an affidavit, subscribed and sworn to before Genevieve D. Scott, Notary Public, Winslow, Arizona, on the 7th day of March, 1953. While he was willing to sign the affidavit, he also told us that he didn't want his name or call letters (since he was a licensed "ham" radio operator) used in any way whatsoever. This was a great disappointment to us, because we felt that without such information any book on the results of the experiments would fall far short of that which we desired for it. The book wouldn't have the authority behind it that we wanted and needed. However, he was a good friend and we told him we would never disclose his name. We are doing so now in this book since Mr. "R" passed away on April 23, 1955, with what was said to be a "heart condition" and "other con-tributing factors."

The Frontispiece of this book contains the original affidavit revealing the names of Mr. "R", licensed com-mercial and amateur radio operator, and his wife, Mrs. "R", plus the name of the Arizona city in which they made their home. Mr. "R" was Lyman H. Streeter, radio oper-ator for the Santa Fe Railroad. His amateur call letters were : W7OJQ. He lived at 423 East Maple Street in Winslow, Arizona.

Lyman had good reasons for not wanting his identity known. First of all, he had never used his call letters during his communication with the space intelligences and he never logged any of his receptions. If these facts were made known, he knew he would lose his license, and this was the last thing he wanted, for to him radio was his very life. Also, he knew that even if he had complied fully with the regulations of the Federal Communications Commission, his license would still be taken away, for no operator is permitted to make contact with an unlicensed operator and, you see, the UFOs aren't licensed with the F.C.C.!

Lyman Streeter's first contact with intelligence from outer

space took place the evening of August 22, 1952. He was a good radio operator holding both a commercial and a "ham" or amateur license. Lyman was very skeptical of the existence of "flying saucers", let alone the possi-bility of communicating with such objects by radio. However, he was willing to attempt contact.

Friday evening, August 22, 1952, Lyman saw what he thought was a very small meteor display over Winslow, Arizona. Then he observed what appeared to be a very bright light traveling at a high altitude in the sky directly above him. He turned on his receiver in his "ham shack" to 400 kc., and immediately, many strange signals were heard but not identified. Later on, the same evening, the Streeters and other witnesses heard strange, clear code signals coming to them as they sat in the main house. Lyman had his "ham shack" on the back of their property, and he had no transmitting or receiving equipment whatsoever in the main house.

At first, everyone thought the signals were coming from the radio shack in the back yard, but when they went to check, there was absolutely nothing to be heard there . . . in fact, the equipment wasn't even turned on. After they came back to the main house the mysterious code was heard again. It seemed to be coming from the very air itself. Since that memorable evening in 1952, many others have reported experiencing exactly the same thing.

About 2:00 a.m., August 23, 1952, code signals were again received. Lyman said it sounded as though two people were talking back and forth to each other, using code . . . but a code unfamiliar to him . It was definitely not standard International Morse Code. The code was coming over his receiver in loud, clear tones. Suddenly, he wrote down a word or two on his note pad: ZO and AFFA. *Anyone who has read THE SAUCERS SPEAK ! A Documentary Report Of Interstellar Communications By Radiotelegraphy knows what those two names mean!*

Later we learned that a superior of Lyman Streeter's in the radio work of the Santa Fe Railroad, a man high up in radio circles, had told him that he also had received strange signals at various times during his radio experiments and that he definitely believed such signals to be from space intelligences. However, he had been evasive when Lyman asked for further information and had seemed to want to discourage him in his own experiments. Why?

One day, this superior called Lyman and told him that Lowell Observatory on Mars Hill in Flagstaff, Ari-zona had observed UFOs on Friday, August 22, 1952. Exactly the same day that Streeter received his first radio signals from space intelligences! This superior also said that a staff member at Lowell Observatory had reported to him earlier that on August 22, 1952, they would focus their large telescope for terrestrial observation over Wins-low, Arizona. But the man had not said what they were going to look for or why. Also, no mention had been made of the source of the information that caused this observation to be made in the first place.

Later, Lyman Streeter had to go to Mars Hill over-looking Flagstaff, Arizona, where he was making a survey for the Santa Fe Railroad in connection with new radio equipment being installed on the top of Mt. Elden. In an area away from the big observatory, he saw a strange, small building surrounded by a high wire fence. Inside the enclosed area he saw two gigantic dogs, obviously being used as watchdogs. Navy men were moving various types of electronic equipment in and out of the little building, which looked new and recently painted. He wondered what electronic equipment was doing on Mars Hill. He was informed that if the new equipment belonging to the railroad being installed on Mt. Elden interfered with the government work on Mars Hill, that it would have to be placed elsewhere!

Several years later we learned that the Government had placed electronic equipment at Lowell Observatory to assist in the tracking of two artificial satellites or space stations that were known to be circling the Earth at four-hundred and at six-hundred miles out in space. In August, 1954, the magazine AVIATION WEEK reported that the two objects were meteors, and insisted that Dr. Linclon La Paz of the University of New Mexico had helped in the identification of them as natural rather than man-made objects. Dr. La Paz attacked the magazine's reference to him, but acknowledged the search for nearby satellites. He also said: "The report is false in every particular insofar as reference to me is concerned." Dr. La Paz and Dr. Clyde Tombaugh, discoverer of the planet Pluto, both worked on the government project at Lowell Observatory, and both of these men are fully aware that the objects tracked by electronic equipment are not natural. and because of their actions in the heavens could only be artificial . . . constructed by other intelligent beings. When Sir Edward Appleton, famous British radio-physicist, said "These two unknown objects are discoveries of great astronomical interest" . . . he didn't know the half of it. Or did he? It is very likely that Sir Edward knew what La Paz and Tombaugh knew, and the same thing that the United States Government knew when it had the Navy set up an experimental station on Mars Hill. Lyman Streeter stumbled into that secret project in 1952 when he was at Lowell Observatory.

It is not the purpose of this book to go into the details of the radio contacts of 1952-53, since these have already appeared in THE SAUCERS SPEAK ! However, one point of great importance which was not brought out in the earlier book, will be taken up in the section entitled Cosmic Rays and a Baby Sun.

Other messages were received, over a period of several months, by Lyman Streeter in his "ham shack" at the back of the lot at 423 East Maple Street in Winslow, Arizona. He had been very skeptical at first. However, after he saw discs in the sky where his radio messages told him to look, discs over his own radio antenna, and after messages were received telling things about which no one but he could have known, and finally, messages coming over the receiver that were answers to questions that had never been transmitted to the intelligences in the usual manner, Streeter's attitude changed. They had either pickd up verbal statements made in the "ham shack" by telepathy and/or by some kind of recording discs. Soon, our Mr. "R" had his proof. I remember his facial expression on many occasions . . . he appeared just too bewildered to even think.

Lyman Streeter usually transmitted on 40 meters and received on 405 kc. On one occasion he received via radiotelephone (voice) on 92 meters. However, we are certain that "frequency" has nothing whatsoever to do with it. Space intelligences have stated many times that they can make anything act as a receiver from radio equipment to the human brain!

At first, Streeter told us that he never had had any interest in UFOs before we contacted him to attempt communication with them. However, upon questioning, he later did admit that he had become very much interested in the possibility of Interstellar Communication in 1950 after he read an article on this subject in "QST", one of the amateur "ham" radio magazines. He said that he had attempted some sort of contact at that time on a high frequency and a short wave length. However, the experiment was a failure and he gave it up.

There was always something strange overshadowing the life of Mr. "R" that I find impossible to describe in words. The only clue I might have would be a radio message from the UFOs we received during the evening of September 28, 1952. At 11 :20 p.m. the following message came through the receiver:

"Radioman has deep secret in his mind. We will not reveal. We are alarmed."

Streeter turned to the rest of us in the "ham shack" and said, "If they (the UFOs) had known about this before, they would never have picked me for your radio-man."

Immediately, code came through the receiver again:

"Be of peace !"

We waited for several minutes without talking until more code started.

"Happy, happy! You, Radioman KANET are installed in the records. Good! Attention! Surprised, my brother?"

What was meant by "deep secret"? Evidently Lyman and his wife knew for they looked at each other in a strange way and she came over to sit beside him and hold his hand. Lyman seemed very concerned over this message. None of us was impolite enough to ask the Streeters what it all meant, so we said nothing. Anyway, the space intelligences didn't stay "alarmed" for long for they spoke of Streeter being "installed in the records" and called him by another name: Radioman KANET ! On page 96 of THE SAUCERS SPEAK! this name was left out of the message because we felt it was something that belonged to Streeter alone and could be of no interest to the public. However, it is well to mention it now for it might be a clue we are looking for!

I remember how one evening Streeter told us, rather reluctantly it seemed, that after attempting contact in 1950 he had appeared one day at work acting in a very strange manner. He went about his assigned radio tasks in the normal way, but his fellow workers noticed he wouldn't answer them when they spoke to him and he acted as if he were in a trance of some kind. His wife was called, and he was taken home. For eight days he was in this unusual "zombie" condition! He said nothing to anyone during that period. Later, when he regained a state of normalcy, he said he couldn't remember a thing that had transpired during those eight days of "amnesia !"

After the contacts started on August 22, 1952, Streeter suddenly remembered what had happened several years previously (during the memory lapse). He told us that he apparently had left his earthly body (that would account for the "zombie" condition ... the physical body had gone about its usual tasks at work under the direction of the "animal mind", while the "entity" had been elsewhere) and awoke in a beautiful large hall where many people were gathering. He was called before a tribunal and no-ticed he was dressed in fine garments . . . he was called by a different name (KANET?)—and told that he must work rapidly to complete his task upon the Earth planet. All he could remember from this eight-day journey was the fact that he must work quickly.

His wife said that before the period of "amnesia" Ly-man was just an ordinary radioman, but after his recovery he spent long hours studying electronics and would work hours on end until he became a very fine radio operator.

Besides working at the Santa Fe radio shop, he had his amateur equipment in his "ham shack" back of his home on Maple Street, and at the other end of this shack he had his workshop where he repaired most of the radios, TV sets, recorders, etc. of the neighborhood, including the car radios of the local Police Department. (I remember that once the Police interrupted one of our communications with the UFOs by driving into the yard one night and asking Lyman to fix their radio. He obliged, but kept trying to hear the code coming in, listen to the idle talk of the officers and fix the radio, all at the same time).

Evidently, Lyman H. Streeter was a "Wanderer" (see p. 206 in the book, OTHER TONGUES-OTHER FLESH) ; his name had been KANET, and he was born on Earth to assist the program of the Space Confederation. His so-called "amnesia" experience must have been his awaken-ing period.

On October 21, 1952, something occurred that was to change the life of Mr. "R". At 8:10 p.m. a small private plane crashed and burned at the airport at Winslow, Ari-zona. This plane was on a mercy flight to a Phoenix hospital with a fourteen-months-old polio victim. All four passengers were instantly killed. One of the workers at the Winslow Timber Company (where Mrs. Streeter also was employed) was working late, and saw the plane take off and minutes later burst into flames. This man told the Civil Aeronautics Administration investigators that immediately after the crash, and before the ambulance and fire truck had arrived, an orange streak sped across the sky and apparerntly landed by the stricken plane! (UFOs appearing at the moment of birth or death is men-tiond in the new book: ROAD IN THE SKY, by G. H. Williamson).

Several days later, a man appeared at the Streeter home and introduced himself as "Mr. Clark." He asked Mrs. Streeter for Lyman and was told that he was out back in the radio shack. The man went out and intro-duced himself to Lyman, saying that although he was not on an official visit, he was with the C.A.A. (Civil Aeronautics Administration) and had just completed his investigations of the crash of October 21st. He showed Lyman his credentials. Then, on a friendlier note, he said:

"I'm a `ham' operator myself."

Then he gave his call letters. (Streeter later checked up and found that there was a "Clark" with the call letters the man had given, but his address was not the same as that which had been given him).

The visitor then sat down, and said bluntly:

"Streeter, what do you think of the flying saucers?"

Lyman sensed something strange underneath all the apparent friendliness, but he answered honestly:

"I have my own personal opinion, if that's what you mean. I think they come from outer space."

And then, very quickly, the man looked Lyman in the eyes and said:

"You've had radio contact with these things, haven't you?"

Streeter realized that this man, "Clark" or whoever he was, knew whether he had had radio communication or not, so he said simply:

"I have conducted certain radio experiments under established scientific procedures . . . yes, I have had con-tact with the flying saucers!"

Whereupon "Clark" asked, "Would you mind show-ing me what you received from them? It's no. secret is it?"

Streeter reached for his notes in a drawer, as he an-swered. "No, it's no secret, I'll be glad to read you what 1 have, but I must tell you that because the messages were sent so fast, I missed many of the words, so the messages are incomplete."

Lyman started to read one message after another. Soon he noticed that whenever he came to a blank space, "Clark" would fill it in! Finally, Streeter said:

"Look here, you must know more about the messages 1

received than I do !"

"That's right," "Clark" answered, "We monitored everything you transmitted and received."

Lyman was startled, to say the least! He said:

"What do you mean by we . . . the government?"

"Clark" hesitated ... put his cigarette out ... looked intently at Lyman for another moment, and then said:

"Of course, who else ?"

Streeter could hardly believe his ears! Confirmation of his experiments at last! But any ideas along this line were soon to be changed rather drastically! Lyman quick-ly answered:

"You mean to tell me, Mr. 'Clark', you admit that flying saucers really exist, are coming from outer space, and that I have personally had radio communication with these objects ?"

"Clark" didn't hesitate in his answers:

"Of course I admit it, but you won't be able to prove it to anyone. You see, no one knows I've been here but you and your wife, and besides, I would never admit we talked about such things. I have been in Winslow strictly for the C.A.A. investigation of the recent plane crash. Remember?"

Weakly, Lyman said:

"Just *what* does your visit to me mean?"

"This is the story," said "Clark": "About the same time you were receiving your coded messages from the extra-terrestrials, fifteen other 'ham' operators through-out the

United States received the same kind of information. We have contacted them all and every one of them is willing to cooperate with his government ... are you?"

Lyman, still unable to believe what was happening answered:

"What do you mean by *cooperation*, Mr. 'Clark'?" Then, the C.A.A. man pulled his "ace-in-the-hole."

"Look, Streeter, we have you dead to rights. You never used your call letters, you never logged your information, and even if you had done all of that, we still can take away your license because you were in communica-tion with unlicensed operators! The F.C.C. (Federal Communications Commission) frowns on such activity you know! Now, you don't want to lose your radio privi-leges; after all, you are commercially licensed besides holding your amateur ticket, and you're making a good living from radio. If your license is taken away, what would you do?"

This was the day Mr. "R" had been dreading. Many times he had told us that there was the possibility of getting in trouble with the F.C.C. because of the unusual nature of the radio experiments. Mr. "Clark" then started "waving the stars and stripes" by saying:

"Lyman, your government is doing all it can to en-lighten the people in connection with the coming of the flying saucers. But the time is not ripe yet. A vast edu-cational program has been planned, and gradually people will come to realize that all space is inhabited, but now the effect would be disastrous if people were to know the truth. Join the other fifteen 'ham' operators and cooper-ate with us. We understand your friends Williamson and Bailey are ready to have a little book published called THE SAUCERS SPEAK! and that it deals with the radio con-tacts ... you know about this, don't you?"

"Yes," said Lyman, "but my name and my city are not

mentioned. No one will be able to locate me from the "account in the book. My friends have promised to leave me out of it."

"That's all right," said "Clark", "but the government doesnt want the radio contact story to be released at this time ... period! You'd better get in contact with Williamson and Bailey and tell them that the book just can't come out at all . . . and be firm about it!"

Lyman answered:

"What can I tell them? I've already given them per-mission to do the story as long as my identity was with-held. They will think it's strange for me to want to stop the book now that it's ready to be distributed !"

"That is your problem, Streeter," said "Clark", "but the story just can't come out now . . . period !" "Clark" went "patriotic" again, and added: "Your government will release such information in due time, but more evi-dence must be accumulated first. Tell your friends that your job is in danger, and your license. Tell them any-thing, but stop that book! We can't contact them, for we have their source of information ... namely you, as radio operator. Besides, if we talk to them it will only give them proof that the entire affair was authentic . . . after all, they may still have a few doubts in the back of their minds. Who knows?"

Streeter was almost speechless, as he said:

"What is expected of me?"

"You must cooperate to the limit with us, but I must warn you," said "Clark," "we will not be able to back you up or support your story in any way whatsoever if you ever tell your contact story or mention my being here today, or our conversation !"

"In other words,' said Lyman, "it will be one-sided cooperation ?"

"In the interests of national security," said "Clark," "Yes, it will be strictly one-sided !"

Mr. "R" had no choice, although "Clark" didn't state it in so many words, it was plain to see that if he didn't cooperate, the F.C.C. regulations would be brought into the picture and he would lose his radio privileges, and, of course, his job with the Santa Fe Railroad! His only an-swer could have been that which it was:

"What is the first step?"

"We want you to increase your power here for trans-mitting," said "Clark". "How soon can you do this and be ready for some experimentation?"

"I can't afford to change my equipment now," said Lyman, "it would be too expensive!"

"We will send you the necessary parts, Streeter," "Clark" said as he rose to go, "but not a word to anyone, and you'd better not give any more information to Wil-liamson and Bailey."

Mr. "Clark" had been sent, not as an official from the F.C.C., for the government felt that would be too severe a shock for Mr. "R" and that he might not give out any information at all. So, they had sent a C.A.A. investigator who was also a "ham" operator, knowing full well that there is a comradeship between all radio amateurs, and this was to serve as the "tie that binds" and so establish communication between "Clark" and Streeter.

Mr. "R" received his needed equipment within a few weeks and started to experiment at once, but never again did he receive anything from the space intelligences after his decision to cooperate with the "powers that be !" Later, he was visited by two officials of the F.C.C. itself who told him to increase his efforts at contact. This he did, there-by affecting many of the neighborhood electronic gadg-ets, so he stopped. He was attempting to beam all mes-sages straight up in a powerful way that would not be needed in ordinary "ham" procedures in contacting other amateurs throughout the world. Why he was told to in-crease his power, I do not know, because while science says that high frequency and high wattage is necessary for any kind of interstellar communication, we know now that power is not important, but that the type wave used is important!

Streeter did call Bailey and he called me in Prescott and asked us to stop the book. Since he had already agreed to our writing the book, I thought he was only worried over the risk of his possible identification, and as I felt quite sure that Lyman was completely safe in our presentation, the book could still come out without any harm to him. Later I was to learn that he was concerned over something else!

I had realized for many weeks that Lyman wasn't acting normally. He avoided us, and while he didn't real-ly seem unfriendly, at the same time he was quite cool .. . as though he knew something that he couldn't tell us. Later we learned that this was true ... due to the fact that he had been visited by Mr. "Clark" . . . who gave his full name as "William (`Bill') Clark." We were quite busy with other UFO happenings, however, about this time. Mr. and Mrs. Bailey and my wife and I were on the desert near Desert Center, California, on November 20, 1952, when George Adamski made his memorable contact with a Venusian. Many people have thought that because of our radio contacts we must have arranged that meeting on the desert, but that is not so, for due to Streeter's new commitments, we were not in radio contact at that time. No arrangements were made beforehand by anyone; we simply went out on the desert and what transpired was completely unexpected by all present.

Many other things of interest happened during December, 1952, January and February, 1953. UFO sightings increased and nature went on a rampage. On December 21, 1952, Lyman Streeter and five other residents of Arizona, observed a large, cigar-shaped object over Winslow. They watched it from 5:00 p.m. until dark. Two smaller UFOs were seen to enter the larger craft and a few minutes later one left the mother-ship. All of this was observed through binoculars.

On February 3, 1953, my wife and I were coming home from downtown Precott, Arizona, when we observed two objects, brighter than the planet Venus, which was in a different position in the sky, come within a few feet of the ground. These craft were close enough that the general "bell-like" outline and the light on top could be easily observed. There was absolutely no sound. I called the U. S. Weather Bureau and was told that there were no planes or balloons in my area. Later the same night I observed another object with an amber light pass very low over my house.

On February 15, 1953, we decided to visit Streeter in Winslow, although at that time we still didn't know about his talk with Mr. "Clark" and we didn't understand his coolness toward us. There were several things we felt needed clearing up in regard to our book, which would shortly be released. We hoped the UFOs would have some ideas or advice for us. We told Lyman that we didn't know whether all the facts should be given to the public or not. He had little to say, for he had already told us that he didn't want the report to come out because of the danger to him and his position. He had the radio receiver turned on, as he always kept it that way when he was in the "ham" shack. He transmitted nothing in connection with our request . . . in fact, he transmitted nothing at all! Suddenly a radio code signal just seemed to "slide in" on 405 kc. At first, Streeter couldn't make any sense out of the dot and dash system used. Finally, one word stood out: "Centuras." This was followed by a very understandable message:

"OK This time it's for you to decide ... We cannot."

The message ended at 12:05 a.m. February 16, 1953. The UFO intelligences would not decide for us . . . we had to do that! So, in THE SAUCERS SPEAK! we gave the account exactly as it happened. We thought perhaps it would have been better to omit the telepathic section of our experiences, for after all it is not untruthful to tell only part of a story! After this communication we felt it best to tell the telepathic experiences as well as the subse-quent radio contacts.

Later, Streeter called me again and told me to stop the presses and prevent the publisher from coming out with the book. I thought this a strange request, for already we had assured him that his identity was hidden. But he said:

"I told you I wanted to be protected, and you didn't live up to your promise because now I hear the book is to be released !"

I told him that we had never agreed to stopping the book, but merely to protecting him, and I said:

"But, Lyman, it will be impossible for anyone to know who you are or where you live . . . you are completely safe."

When he still insisted that we stop the book, by force if need be, I became very suspicious, and started an investigation which led to my discovery of the Mr. "Clark" episode you have just read. Previously, he had agreed to our writing the book provided that he be left out of it, but suddenly when the book is practically in the hands of the public, he does a quick turn-about. Something was wrong somewhere! I wanted to know what . . . and I found out: First, one visitor in the form of "Clark" and then two more men from the F.C.C. There is little doubt in my mind that Lyman H. Streeter had been visited by the notorious "three men in black !"

A. David Middelton, who has a wide and varied background in electronics and the communication field decided to investigate Mr. "R". Somehow he learned his identity, and personally interviewed Streeter. Middelton is a Senior Member of the Institute of Radio Engineers and was formerly a director of the American Radio Relay League. He holds an Extra Class Amateur License and maintains W5CA. Middelton was a project engineer at Fort Monmouth during World War II and also a civilian radar field engineer attached to the U. S. Navy. Moving to A.R.R.L. headquarters, he was Assistant Editor of QST, and later corresponding Editor of CQ magazine. Currently, Mr. Middelton is working for the United States Government in electronics.

In January, 1955, Mr. Middelton (W5CA) discussed the radio contacts with Lyman Streeter in person in Winslow, Arizona. Later, I provided additional details. "After full consideration of all data," said Mr. Middelton, "it is my opinion that these contacts were made by Mr. 'R' as described."

About the same time, early in 1955, Mr. Middelton received reports Of radio contact established between UFOs and a VE3 radio operator in Canada. He stated at the time that he "believed the contacts were authentic al-though technical details were lacking." The question Mr. Middelton asked, and rightly so, was:

"Why have bonafide amateur UFO contact data been conspicuous by their absence in 'ham' discussions on and off the air? Gould it be that the amateurs involved have been afraid to report such contacts (QSOs) ? Afraid of what, or whom? Or, maybe there just have not been UFO amateur contacts other than the W7 and VE3 experi-ences!"

Because of Mr. "Clark's" statement about the fifteen other amateur radio operators, we know there were more than W7 and VE3. That leaves us with: "Afraid of what, qr whom?"

After examining the facts in regard to Lyman Streeter's contacts, Mr. Middelton wrote the following letter:

Federal Communications Commission
Amateur Division, Washington, D. C.

April 9,1955

Dear OMs .

This is a formal and serious inquiry.

In view of information reaching me from serious-ly interested sources, the situation might arise where-in an amateur operator, duly licensed and operating within the amateur bands of this country, might be called by a station purporting to be from Outer Space or from Unidentified Flying Objects. Such stations also operating in our bands.

The call signs used by these UFOs are not any more unusual than many of the strange and weird ones being assigned by some foreign countries, I understand. In view of this fact, it would be difficult to ascertain if the station was, in fact, just another DX country, or one not on this planet, as far as the call sign is concerned.

Will you please inform me as to the feelings and desires of the Amateur Division of the FCC on this matter, if any. Also, will you please inform me of regulations covering this matter?

I realize that this is a strange inquiry but it is definitely in order, and made in a sincere effort to ascertain the FCC views on this matter.

Also, what about amateurs transmitting within our authorized bands but receiving on frequencies outside the bands . . . this too is of concern. This involves QSOs wherein the amateur did not make the call up.

I would appreciate having your reply to this mat-ter, with any degree of secrecy you wish to place on it.

Respectfully yours,
(Signed) A. DAVID MIDDELTON, W5CA

Mr. Middelton wanted to "ascertain FCC views on the matter," and that's exactly what the FCC didn't want him to do. Mr. Middelton's high reputation in this field, and the fact that his technical articles have been widely ac-claimed in radio circles and reprinted throughout the world, didn't do very much to convince the FCC they could answer him "with any degree of secrecy" at all! He received a letter from them as follows:

FEDERAL COMMUNICATIONS COMMISSION
WASHINGTON 25, D. C. April 25, 1955
File: 7400

A. David Middelton
Tijeras, New Mexico

Dear Sir:
This is in reference to your letter of April 9, 1955, requesting comments concerning regulations which would apply to possible communications with uniden-tified flying objects.

In regard to amateur radio stations, Section 12.101, of Part 12 of the Commission's Rules Governing Amateur Radio Service specifies the points of communications permitted for amateur stations li-censed by the Commission.

Within the limitations of Section 12.101, amateurs may communicate with stations which trans-mit on frequencies outside the amateur frequency bands.

Very truly yours,
(Signed) MARY JANE MORRIS
Secretary

Between the time Mr. Middelton wrote to the FCC on April 9th, and the time he received an answer from Wash-ington on April 25th, Lyman H. Streeter (Mr. R.) had passed away on April 23, 1955. The death certificate read : ". . . heart condition . and other contributing factors."

Needless to say, the extreme mental anxiety and pressure placed upon Lyman Streeter didn't exactly place him in a state of exuberant 'health. He was a very young man to die . . . but I feel certain that "Kanet," the radio-man, had done his job . . . had completed the mission he came here to do. Who is to say? Surely not the FCC!

THE SILENCE GROUP

How did the government know Lyman Streeter was experimenting? Monitoring stations couldn't possibly have known of every detail of his work as Mr. "Clark" evidently did. Is it possible that Streeter's superior, in whom he confided and who told him of the secret project at Lowell Observatory, reported his activities? If so, to whom? And why? These are questions to which we may never have the answers. And what was the "deep secret" in connection with the life of Streeter that the UFOs were so concerned about?

There is more to UFO visitations than any man yet knows, but a definite pattern is beginning to emerge and it staggers the mind! The true purpose for present space visitation may actually be millions of miles from us out in that same space. An explanation of this statement will appear in the next section of this book when we speak of the increase in cosmic rays.

Information we have collected on the "Super Government" or "Hidden Empire" is of such importance and magnitude that it must be presented to the public at once! After reading THEY KNEW Too MUCH ABOUT FLYING SAUCERS, by Gray Barker, many pieces of a previously incomplete puzzle fell into place.

In his Epilogue, Barker said: "If these strange visit-ors do not represent governmental authorities, then what fantastic sponsorship is responsible for their deeds?" Barker was, of course, referring to the "three men" who paid Albert Bender a visit under mysterious circum-stances and advised him to discontinue his "Saucer" investigatoins.

Barker continued: "As yet I do not have that answer . . . I

wish I did." We do have that answer, and it imme-diately explains another enigma : THE SILENCE GROUP!

On page 234, Barker refers to this group when he writes: ". . . it looks pretty obvious from here just who working for . . . the people you and I both know exist, but would give our right arms to have the real dope on." Barker goes on to say that everyone in "SAUCERS" knows of the existence of The Silence Group, but no one as yet has put a finger on just what it is or who makes up the group.

Some individuals may feel that Barker's book is too frightening . . . that such material shouldn't be presented to the public in these times of great world unre' However, Barker does a magnificent job of straight reporting. Fortunately, none of his "pet" theories or opinions are to be found in the book. He merely gives us facts and lets us decide for ourselves. The book can be credited as being one of the first to bring to light the strange and sometimes terrifying happenings behind-the-scenes in UFO research. On page 246 Barker says that he is not alarmed about bug-eyed monsters, little green men, or hostile "Saucers". He says that something else disturbs him far more:

"There exists forces or agencies which would prevent us from finding out whether or not there are such green men, or bug-eyed monsters, or saucers with things in them. I have a feeling that some day there will come a slow knocking at my own door. They will be at your door, too, unless we all get wise and find out who the three men really are."

Barker mentions several things which give us a clue to the identity of the mysterious visitors. On page 123, referring to Bender, he says: "Whoever the three men were, they didn't want him to think any longer, or to encourage others to think."

On page 205, he quotes from "Gordon Smallwood's" letter.

"Smallwoods", referring to the man who paid him a visit, says: "The man wasn't representing what I thought him to be representing. There is certainly no government agency involved . . . the man who came to see me threatened me very openly . . ."

Barker comments on the above by saying: "If the visitor was not from Smallwood's government, I reasoned, what agency could he represent? Were private individuals engaged in suppressing the facts? Were certain agencies, opposed to saucer investigation, operating?"

The visitors who call upon "saucer" researchers and advise them strongly to give up their work do not want these men to "think or encourage others to think" ... they represent "no government agency" . . . they "threaten openly."

The "three men" are not just peculiar to "Saucer" in-vestigation, for there have always been "three men" pres-ent during every great event of recorded (and unrecorded) history. They operate as hired henchmen of the "International Bankers" and their only duty is to suppress all men who would act as channels of truth to other men.

Many people have asked the inevitable question: "If visitors from other worlds are here, why doesn't our government inform us of such a momentous event?" The reason is obvious . . . all governments, yes all, are under the complete control of the "International Bankers" who also control all money and thus create depressions and prosperity whenever they want it. They want and need a *divided* world so that wars may continue and their wealth steadily increase. The term "Bankers" is a vague one .. . but the powerful individuals who really run the world's governments can be named!

We suggest that those of you who are really interested in duplicating the "job" our forefathers did in 1776, and want to see the United States of America fulfill its proper destiny, write to (The authors are in no way connected with the Cinema Educational Guild, Inc., nor do they ac-cept all the policies of this organization. However, enough material from this source definitely points its "finger" at the "International Bankers" and their conspiracy).: Cinema Educational Guild, Inc., P. O. Box 46205, Cole Br., Hollywood 46, California. It is organized to combat one thing: Communism. The force behind the "International Bankers" who constitute the "Hidden Empire" stems from Communist Russia. Write to the Cinema Educational Guild and ask for their material . . . you will be shocked, as any true American should be!

Here are two paragraphs from their Booklet No. 49, OUR SECRET GOVERNMENT :

"The individuals who compose our 'secret govern-ment' are, of course, invisible to the public eye. Bernard Baruch, Felix Frankfurter, Herbert Lehman, the War-burgs are unquestionably top figures in the Great Con-spiracy, but not even Baruch is the hierarch of the Cabal. He is the 'Field Commander.' He and his above-men-tioned affiliates choose the top tool such as FDR was, such as Ike is today; they choose the lower tools, such as Harry Dexter White, Dean Acheson, Alger Hiss . . . and they dictate all lower job appointments. They are the `they' Ike meant when he said: had to say `yes' because they told me they didn't have time to build up another candidate.' They are the men who set up Ike's 'Advisory Staff' during World War Two . . . they are the men who set up his Advisory Staff, better known as the 'Palace Guard', after he was elected to the Presidency.

"Every one of these individuals (of the 'Palace Guard' owes his place in the sun to the Internationalist Cabal."

Every king, president or dictator on Earth is only a figure-head . . . a tool of the "Hidden Empire." For millennia this group has been determined to keep truth from mankind for selfish purposes! They have removed vital books and sections of the Holy Bible until it is unrecog-nizable . they have written history as they wished to, not as it really happened . . . they wave flags and scream: "Patriotism !" and thousands of young men, women and children die so that vast war machines may be fed. But mankind is waking up! Men are no longer content to re-main "stupid" and believe what they are told to believe. It matters not whether the "authority" is religious, political, or otherwise, for there is only one hierarchy . . . the "In-ternational Bankers."

These secret world rulers will never allow official UFO announcemenTs to be made to the public. If they did allow it, it would spell their doom. If the technology of the space visitors is revealed it will immediately eliminate the need for oil, gas, automobiles, and practically every-thing else that drains the public and keeps every family in America on a credit-buying spree until they are deposited six feet under.

When space intelligences tell the people of the world how magnificently life is lived on other worlds, the men who have been dictating our way of life to us for so long are going to be on the spot ... their "Hidden Empire" will be "hidden" no longer ... it will crumble away in the light of a New Dawn . . . truly, even the "mountains and hills will not give them shelter."

In 1947 "Flying Saucers" first came to public attention in our generation. This last decade (1947-1957) has been termed the "Haunted Decade." And, indeed, it has been "haunted" for more reasons than just the appearance of UFOs. I believe we have men on Earth scientifically capable of being able to tell us what the UFOs are, after ten long years of investigation. Yet, nothing comes from officialdom. No acceptance! No denial! The governments of the world have done next to nothing in educating the public with regard to life on other worlds (which they know exists) and the more important fact that such life is sending space craft to Earth at the present time. The only answer for such stupidity is the International Cabal.

We suggest you write to your Senators and Congressmen . . . not because the Government may be forced to make some official statement, but to make these public servants aware of the UFO situation. (Many know noth-ing about space visitation since they are caught up in the whirl of Washington society . . . vote getting, etc.). Help the men you elected to office to do a better job for themselves and for you and your neighbor. Flood them with letters and more letters, asking them to look into UFO in-vestigation . . . demand a Congressional Hearing on all the facts!

At the present time, Wayne S. Aho, former Major, U. S. Army Combat Intelligence officer, is heading Washington Saucer Intelligence, P. O. Box 815, Washington 4, D. C. Write to him and give him your support as he works amongst the men on Capitol Hill. The America envisioned by men like Washington and Jefferson is gone ... enslaved by the Internationalists! Benjamin Franklin said: "Gentlemen, we give you a Republic . . . now try and keep it !" Unfortunately, we have not kept it . . . it has been lost in the Reddest Treason of the Reddest Star in our section of the Universe . . . the planet Earth!

Major Donald E. Keyhoe has devoted two books to the subject of the Silence Group . . . yet no one in UFO research, including Keyhoe, really knows exactly what that enigmatic term means. Keyhoe felt that perhaps the men comprising this group weren't especially malevolent because of their "tell nothing" policy, but were merely doing what they felt certain was best for the average citizen. We say that their intentions are anything but kindly .. . they serve an ancient, hideous conspiracy that is nothing but the spirit of Anti-Christ!

The servants of such evil see to it that the public is constantly deluged with movies, radio, TV, magazines, etc., touting the great merits of body-destroying liquor, tobacco, immorality! They wish to weaken us to the point where we offer no resistance to their propaganda of lies. It is a vast campaign with the ultimate domination of the human race, physically, mentally and spiritually as its "noble" goal.

Get yourself, your family and your loved ones and friends on a simple, natural diet. This is not fanaticism. It is good common sense, for the "Hidden Empire" is deliberately placing dangerous elements in the world's food supply! You say all of this sounds incredible. Then investigate for yourself and do something about it.

There is practically no such thing in this country to-day as natural food. Few people realize it, but chemicals are used at every point in food processing from field to table! Chemical additives are used in stabilizers, preservatives, disinfectants, antioxidants, extenders (quantity increasers), tenderizers, emulsifiers, growth-promoters, fumigants, herbicides, defoliants (hair removers), fungicides, miticides (mite killers), bleaches, sweeteners, con-ditioners, colorants, to improve flavor, etc., etc. Chemicals are used in curing meats; textures of many products such as ice cream, are improved by such chemicals as polyoxy-ethylene derivatives; canned tomatoes and apple slices, which tend to fall apart, are improved by additions of small amounts of certain calcium salts; some companies keep a head on beer with cellulose gum; even the appetizing color of asparagus soup may be simply color added for eye appeal!

Biological science can now control the emotional na-ture of man through the use of certain chemicals in his food supply... the emergence of new and deadly chemicals into the food of the world is overwhelming and terrifying. What drastic step will the Internationalists take next?

Refuse to be a part of this evil scheme to destroy man on Earth . . . physically, mentally and spiritually! Eat only natural food! The Cabal will stop at nothing in its last stand against the forces of Truth. Is that not sufficient reason for eating food the way it was created by the Infinite One?

In Communist Russia, homes are entered in the early hours of the morning and the unwilling occupants who have somehow offended the "powers that be" are dragged away from the security of their own families to be placed in faraway institutions for the insane. Now the Internationalists are bold enough to attempt the very same thing in America!

On January 18, 1956, the House of Representatives passed with a voice vote and without objections, House Bill No. 6376. (This Bill was later radically changed, so that most of its frightening features were eliminated when it reached the Senate. But this was due to the fact that thousands upon thousands of letters poured into your elected representatives in Washington, D. C., demanding that this anti-American document be stopped or completely altered. That's why we say: "Write your Congress-man and your Senator before it's too late !).

This bill provides for and designates 1,000,000 acres in Alaska for the establishment of a hospital for the mentally ill ... an insane asylum. On the surface that sounds relatively harmless except it might appear that one mil-lion acres is a rather large piece of ground to house the approximately 350 known mental cases in Alaska. This is an area larger than the entire State of Rhode Island! The bill further provides for the expenditure of $12,500,- 000 over a ten-year period. The subtle wording of this bill makes it appear on the surface as a piece of philanthropic legislation, but careful study reveals it to be vicious and against the basic rights of man.

For instance, a mentally ill individual is defined in Section 101 (i) as follows: "An individual having a psy-chiatric or other disease which subsequently impairs his mental health or an individual who is mentally defective or mentally retarded."

This is rather a broad definition . . . it could include anyone who reads this book! Certain interested parties would have the prerogative of putting a citizen in that institution from which escape would be nearly impossible. Red tape has been cut to facilitate incarceration. If we displease the "powers that be" in any way whatsoever, *our free speech could cost our liberty!*

We haven't the space here to go into all the details of this incredible bill, but it gives the individual citizen no say whatsoever ... he could be dragged from his home on the flimsiest excuse! Newspapers, radio and other sources of public information, have been quiet about House Bill No. 6376 just as they are quiet abcut UFOs . . . pressure has been exerted from the Internationalists!

Innocent, mentally well Americans are to be railroaded into an arctic insane asylum? Keyhoe called it: *The Flying Saucer Conspiracy . . . but it's more, much more . . . a conspiracy against God and Man!*

No wonder Bender was frightened. Is it not significant that he wasn't particularly afraid of the "secret of the Saucers," but only became terrified after the vi*sit of the "three men"? Therefore, it wasn't the origin or* cause of the "Saucers" that caused him to be ill but the *reason why* all governments are prevented from making any offi-cial public statements in regard to the UFOs.

For many months now we have been reaching some conclusions. Are they the same conclusions that Bender reached? Let us *suppose* for a moment that the following happened:

Through research let us say, Bender discovered that the "Saucers" were *interplanetary*. That was the *origin*. But more important to the people of Earth was the cause. He then discovered that our planet, even our entire Solar System was being absorbed into a gigantic embryonic star. Earth was on a "collision course" with a *sun*. What man wouldn't be startled!

Soon Bender found ample proof for such a theory in strange weather phenomena, the melting polar ice cap at the North Pole, the increased cosmic ray bombardment, etc. (See : Other Tongues—Other Flesh by G. H. Williamson) .

In his book (page 174), Gray Barker writes: "The swifter accumulation of ice (at the South Pole) is perhaps due to a part of space the Earth is now passing through ... cosmic ray bombardment, directed mainly at the 'top' of the Earth, where the ice cap at the North Pole is melt-ing, may have something to do with it."

According to some scientists, there is the ever-present possibility that the Earth will "flip" on its axis! This, of course, would completely destroy civilization and almost all life on the planet.

All the foregoing, however, are effects, but perhaps it was the cause that worried Bender. That cause was the gigantic sun that was drawing many worlds toward its center like a powerful, monstrous whirlpool.

Bender realized what this meant to humanity . . . he had discovered the origin and cause of the UFOs . . . yet, he felt there was hope, for friendly planetary neighbors were here, evidently to assist us in this period of crisis. As our Sun, which is their Sun also, moves deeper into the danger area of space there is the ever-presnt possibility that it will explode. You see, our Sun is an orange dwarf star, and such suns have the nasty habit of doing just that.

Bender realized that space visitors were here in

everincreasing numbers to prepare for this event . . . an event which may eventually necessitate the evacuation of an entire Solar System. Fantastic? Yes! But remember, Bender and the others used that word over and over again .. . fantastic, fantastic!

Bender felt he must reveal his discoveries to the public, for while catastrophe was imminent, still mankind should be overjoyed because "salvation was nigh" in the form of our arriving space visitors. Barker writes that the coming of the "Saucers" is both good and bad for mankind. The bad is the reason why they have to come, and the good is the fact that they are coming!

Then the "three men" came, and Bender learned the truth about our world ... that it is a "prison world" where men are pawns in the mad game of the "Hidden Empire" . . . it was this startling fact, revealed to Bender by his visitors that shocked and sickened him ... or was it? We don't know for sure, because Bender has never said. How-ever, certain facts are quite obvious!

In THE SAUCERS SPEAK! radiotelegraphic contact with space intelligence brought to light the fact that our Earth was "listing" (page 87) and that a "very poor condition exists" (page 88). "We cannot stand by and see another waste of creation . . . this can be the end of all on Saras (Earth)" (page 89).

Those statements fit our "supposition" above! Were the references to that gigantic sun? Were the UFOs thinking of the effects on our planet?

We have already mentioned the radio message of September 28, 1952, when the UFO intelligences spoke of the "deep secret" in the mind of Lyman Streeter. This was before his late October, 1952, contact with Mr. "Clark". Lyman Streeter was evidently contacted by a "visitor" who showed "credentials." The pattern was so familiar to Bender and others. Who visited Streeter at that early date? What did they tell him that made him appear so strangely terrified?

Information that has been accumulated over a period of many months now makes more sense than it ever had before. The happenings of 1952-53 during our radiotelegraphic experiments (even the strange burning odor made its appearance); the visitors who approached our radio operator, Lyman Streeter; the statement made on radio by space intelligences; the fantastic facts about our poles and the great sun; the Silence Group and the "International Bankers" . . . all these seemingly unrelated facts suddenly added up to the most fantastic (is there any other word?) story of all time! And the most closely guarded secret of all time, I might add.

On page 227, Barker writes: " 'D. C. is practically a police state,' a prominent saucer book author was telling me over coffee in his Washington home. 'I'm moving away from here as quickly as I can. I could tell you more but you wouldn't believe it'."

On page 226, we read: "Saucer enthusiasts wondered just what 'some other organization' might imply, since the dreadful possibility that some such power might exist was in effect being acknowledged by a noted academic leader."

Such power does exist! The "Hidden Empire" will not remain "'hidden" much longer, but it will go down in defeat, as Truth alone is victorious. We have the promise of our God that this shall be so.

The Silence Group will never allow UFO information to officially reach the public. Therefore, the UFOs are literally pushing the man on the street into a conscious-ness where he can accept the inhabitation of space . . . space ships . . . and space people. Man on Earth has longed for a one world for so long that the International-ists decided to give him their own special conception .. . the United Nations. The U. N. has wilfully and deliberately plotted to transform itself into a super One World Government that would absorb the United States, destroy our sovereignty and void and nullify our Constitution! Don't be fooled by the U.N., for it is Anti-Christ from first to last. These are the prophecied times when even the "elect" might be deceived.

A fine book that has been out of print is available again:

THE SECRET WORLD GOVERNMENT by General Count Cherep-Spiridovich. You can obtain it from Women's Voice, Room 805, 537 South Dearborn Street, Chicago, Illinois.

Also get. THE CRIME AGAINST HUMANITY (it tells about cancer being deliberately caused in Americans by Americans). You can get it from the Humanitarian Society, Clyde Barr, Route 2, Fayetteville, Arkansas. During the past three years, through the aid of the Federal Government bureaucracy with local and State complicity, the medical and drug monopoly has been making a pawn of the sick folks of America. Under the guise of looking after your interests they are taking away your constitutional freedom in matters of health, which when accomplished will make Americans subject to their every whim! Freedom of choice is your American heritage! Write to the National Health Federation, 2454 Van Ness Avenue, San Francisco 9, California for startling informaton dealing with your health birthright!

Of course, there are many other reports if you care to investigate. In the name of Almighty God *look up* and *wake up!*

COSMIC RAYS AND A BABY SUN

The inevitabe question seems to be: "When and where will the UFOs land on Earth?"

To answer this, it is best to give the statements made by space intelligences themselves. When they were asked what they would do to prevent an atomic war on Earth, the exclaimed: "We will do absolutely nothing to prevent or stop such a war!"

They have stated that they do not know whether there will be such a civilizaTion-destroying war or not. However, they point to the fact that all ancient prophecy, whether found the Holy Bible, in other sacred books, or in manuscripts, etc., definitely indicates that there will be a conflict of such magnitude that our present civilization will collapse completely.

They have stated in numerous authentic contacts that if we decide on peace and follow a true One World Policy, they will eventually land, share some of their great developments with us, and assist us in taking our rightful place in the Interplanetary Brotherhood. They have further stated that if we do not decide on peace, and a great atomic war emerges, they will not interfere but will let such a war progress to the stage where it can no longer be effectively waged due to the fact that both sides have been defeated by the total ruin of technical organization.

Some of you might ask : "But if the space people are here to help us, why will they allow such a frightful war to continue, or even start in the first place?"

We must remember that according to Universal Law, our space visitors cannot interfere with our progress on Earth.

Since the Earth is only a classroom in the Father's many mansions certain lessons must be learned before Earthman earns graduation to higher spheres. An eighth grader doesn't enter the first grade to make fun of the stu-dents because they do things more simply than himself. Likewise, spacemen aren't going to step in and dictate to us ... they are going to let us learn our lessons in our own way, even though they will undoubtedly be very painful lessons for the history of the Earth has proven this to be always true on this "sorrowful" planet!

Space mentors declare, however, that the world is not going to end, even though there will be terrain changes, and violent storms, etc., still man is only to inherit the beautiful and good on Earth. After millennia this planet has managed to produce a "harvest" of souls who can live in fellowship, love and peace with their fellow men. It is this "harvest" or "remnant" that shall inherit the "New Earth" of the "Golden Dawn.'

I do not support the "prophet of doom predictions that claim our world will be utterly destroyed by fantastic power, etc. But that there will be great destruction locally in various parts of the Earth there is no question! Yet will it not be worth it, if we awaken to a New Earth, purified and cleansed of all lust, greed and war? Is this not the Great Dream of all ages?

You ask : "But what about the millions who will perish? Is this not a terrible loss?"

Let us remember that life is eternal ... therefore no one will actually "perish" ... they will only leave a planet that is no longer suitable for their development. Those who haven't learned the lessons contained in the Sermon on the Mount will be reborn on other worlds where they will remain until they do learn Universal Laws and how to apply them. The space intelligences do not look upon "death" the same way we do. If we are born to die, then we must also die to live! Why are the UFOs here? It is a difficult ques-tion to answer, but is usually summed up in the following :

1. Atomic experiments on Earth and our advance-ment in eventual space travel and the exploration of space have alerted other inhabited planets. (There is always an increase in UFO sightings and "fireball" phenomena after atomic experiments and the launching of "sputniks.")
2. This is the psychological time for outer space in-telligences to make their appearance on Earth due to the above (No. 1) reason.

3. The space visitors wish to assist the "remnant" on Earth after catastrophe and return the Earth to the Interplanetary Brotherhood from which it fell countless generations ago.
4. They (UFOs) are fulfilling prophecy concerned with the approaching "New Age", "Great Cycle" or "Second Coming."
5. 5. Space friends intend to evacuate large portions of Earth's population in the event the axis of Earth shifts. (Read page 238 of INSIDE THE SPACE SHIPS by Adamski).

Apparently the above reasons sum up the main pur-poses for the coming of the UFOs. However, for some time, I have been aware that there is a much bigger and even greater purpose behind it all that the UFOs have not yet revealed in any contacts! Although they show great love toward us, why have they decided to put on a mass appearance at this time? What are they educating us for? If we are progressing in our own classroom why should they disturb us at all? What great cosmic change or knowledge of it has prompted them to come now?

At first, the man in the street wants to know if there are,

indeed, "little orange balls going that-away!" Once he is convinced that something is "going that-away" .. . then he wants to have the greater answer: Why are. "little orange balls going that-away?"

In some contacts, a great "dust cloud" has been mentioned, and the fact that our Earth is now in the outer fringes of this area. Undoubtedly, by "dust cloud" they are referring to a great cosmic "cloud" or area of intense cos-mic ray activity that not only our Earth is entering, but our entire Solar System.

Evidently, for centuries, scientists of other worlds have realized that our Solar System was heading directly for the center of this cosmically disturbed area, and they knew what would happen when the Earth and its neigh-bors plunged deeper and deeper into this "dark cloud" of space! Yes, we are now on the outer fringes of a great field . . . "cloud" . . . of energy, and we are experiencing the first effects in the form of strange weather, melting polar ice caps, earthquakes ,increased cosmic ray bom-bardment and the effect on radio broadcasting, etc. The latter was brought to the public's attention some months ago. The governments of the world have been aware of this change for some time and are deeply concerned. Special projects have been set up to study radiation and its effect on organic life, etc.

Project "Rome" was set up to study the magnetic ef-fects at our North and South Poles. Since a planet is a "space ship" itself, what better way to investigate the "Universal Energy" that powers such a craft, than to study the force at its source . . . the polar vents of the Earth it-self ! Project NQ-707 was set up to attempt communica-tion with the UFOs (at Edwards Ar Force Base, Cali-fornia).

In 1955-56 I was in correspondence with a wellknown foreign scientist who said that after intensive research by government scientists they came to a terrifying conclusion ...

and that was that our planet is moving very rapidly on a collision course with a gigantic embryonic sun!

Research in this country by men like Dr. Kurt Sitte, Syracuse University, and Dr. Jason J. Nassau, Director of Warner-Swasey Observatory, Cleveland, Ohio, and others shows us that, indeed, the electron count has speeded up and the cosmic ray bombardment increased fantastically! The International Science Symposium held recently in Rome, Italy, reached incredible conclusions!

What does this "collision course" really mean to the people of the world? First of all, relax, for it very defi-nitely does not mean the end of the world. Eventually, perhaps centuries from now man will have to leave the Earth, his old home for the last few million years, and mi-grate through interstellar space to a new home. But for our generation and time we are told we must not be con-cerned with the world ending! A New Golden Age is about ready to be born on the Earth and the planet beneath our feet will have to be here, indeed, if we are to reap the glorious benefits of such a New Age! However, as we plunge deeper into the magnetic field of the new baby sun, the effects will become more noticeable . . . this will increase as time goes on ... more terrain changes, etc.

The most closely guarded secret of all time is not that visitors from Outer Space are here on Earth, but why they are here! They have come to prepare us for a new tech-nology and age on our world so that we might be ready for the eventual journey through space that defies. description! We are gathering data all the time on this and it will be presented as we receive and study it!

Unfortunately, our designated "superiors" and "authorities" are not preparing us for anything! It is rather obvious that politicians aren't going to help us ... neither are militarists, scientists nor religionists!

Noted astronomers are certain there is life on Mars. Great areas. change from brown to green with the seasons and other blue-green areas change in tint. This is good evidence of vegetation or plant life. But what about more intelligent beings? Astronomers know beyond the shad-ow of a doubt that a great intelligent race of beings exists on Mars because photographs taken during research in 1954 prove the existence of the canals, and more important still . . . prove they are artificial . . . constructed by men like ourselves!

Scientists have had ample time since 1947, when the UFOs were first given widespread publicity, to do an about-face on their "lifeless universe" theory. They could have saved face by suddenly telling the public that through their great discoveries they had found intelligent life existing on neighboring worlds! No one, in the excite-ment, would remember that until the announcement was made science had refused to accept such a belief! However, propaganda in the hands of an expert works wonders with masses of people! For example, remember how millions of Americans suddenly had their minds changed for them during World War II . . . "Bloody Joe" (Stalin) became "Uncle Joe", and we had to learn to love Russia . a country we formerly were told Ito hate. After World War II, the public had its mind changed again, and the allies we needed during the war, had to become the hated ones again!

Once man had accepted life outside his own puny Earth, he would have been ready for the greater revelation : Not only is there life out in space, but it is now coming to Earth in the UFOs!

But there have been no statements from the "priestly" scientists! Will they reveal their discoveries about Mars, the Moon, etc.? They will not! Any astronomer who has dared to make a public statement has been literally "shut up" by having the "security curtain" dropped over him!

The UFOs are here to help us wake up. They are the fulfillment of all ancient prophecy in that they remind us that "our salvation draweth nigh !" The religious leaders of the world and their churches have done practically nothing about informing their flocks of the importance of the coming of the discs. That the UFOs tie in with prophetic statements of the Bible, etc. there is no question! Then what's the matter with the clergy of the world? They are men of God who are supposed to bring Truth to the hungry "sheep" of the Lord!

But are they really men of God? "By their fruits ye shall know them" the Bible tells us. So, let's examine the "fruit" of the clergy for a moment. If they (and by "they" we mean any religious leader in any denomination) really belive in Jesus the Christ and really believe what He taught as Divine teaching, then why don't they interpret His words correctly? During World War II ministers on both sides were heard to say : "God is surely on our side, so you young men go out and fight hard for your country, your freedom and your Creator!" This is simply the ancient pagan idea that God at various times takes sides and allows one group of men to kill and maim another group of men. It's the kind of theology that holds up a bloody god of war and death as the Supreme Intelligence of the Universe . . . an "all-loving" God! How contradictory can they get? This is not inspiration from God ... this is simply the mouthing of "patriotic drivel" thought up by the Internationalists . . . the warmongers who profit on dead bodies of the innocent!

God takes no sides! Christ does not, and could not condone any war! Here is a challenge : Let the self-appointed "priests" of this world tell all men everywhere that because Christ said "turn your cheek," "meet hate with love," "love your enemies," "he that takes up the sword will surely die by the sword," "do good to them that hate you," etc., etc., they (the men of Earth) should never take up arms again to destroy their fellowmen!

If the world's great Christian religious leaders would tell mankind that it is utterly and completely against the teachings of Jesus the Christ to fight and kill, do you think a successful war could be waged? What if such an order came from the Vatican? What if a Catholic would suffer excommunication for becoming a soldier or even for en-gaging in defense activities? A great number of potential fighting men in the world's population would be lost to the cause of the "Hidden Empire" wars.

But apparently people believe what they are told, and in many cases they don't want to think ... it's much easier to let someone else do that! How many times have we seen paintings of Jesus with outstretched hands bestowing blessings on servicemen girded to the loins with all kinds of devilish devices for taking the life of a brother .. another spark of Divine Life?

The fault may lie at the door of the Emperor Constan-tine and his conclave of bishops and priests. This ruler in 325 A.D. assembled at Nicaea in Bithynia, a great council of over three hundred prelates, representing the differ-ent Christian churches throughout the Roman Empire and its satellites. They put into binding circulation certain dogmas, creeds and doctrines for the followers of the humble Christ. Therefore, a military emperor put his imperial signature to documents that were to affect most powerfully the destinies of the Christian nations . . . in-deed, the whole world!

A military man cannot suddenly be called to the role of "Dove of God" or "Dove of Peace." Today, the so-called "rulers" of Earth are nothing but the "puppets" of the International Cabal. Go to the polls and vote and you don't vote for this man or that ... for no matter who is elected, only one power is going to be in control anyway . . . the same power that has been in control since man came to Earth and knew the difference between "good and evil !" It is the same power that made Constantine hide his bloody battle armour and act out the role of Christ's representative on Earth!

The Bible and other sacred 'books have been changed until they are no longer recognizable. So, man has been enslaved by the powers of darkness on this strange little planet. But the time is fast approaching (in fact, is it not here?) when men will no longer look to priests and kings, to scientists lost in their own imagin-ings, to "authority" wherever it exists! Man has access to the throne of God himself. He needs no one to "save" him from anything. Do not listen to the "mouthpieces" of the "Hidden Empire" . . . the politicians who promise you this or that for your physical existence . . . the priests who promise you life everlasting and eternal glory if you follow them . . . the generals who exist only because of war and suddenly are presented "holy" before you as "god-fearing," "righteous" men . . . scientists who promise to give you immortality from a test-tube when you already are an immortal being!

"Howbeit in vain do they worship me, teaching for doctrines the commandments of men." (Mark 7:7).

Those who would place themselves over you as your guardians are teaching you the "commandments of men" and are passing them off as the "doctrines of God!" Wake up! In the name of an all-loving and compassionate Creator, *wake up!*

The quicker we realize that this is *"revolution"*, the quicker the job will be done and the "Kingdom of Heaven" established upon the Earth! Yes, this is revolution . . . it is a revolt against tyranny, greed, lust, war, hatred and opposition to the basic rights of all men! Let us not be found wanting . . . stand with your Creator and not with the forces of darkness we have talked about in this book. "If God is with us, who can be against us?"

Recently, I heard a well-known radio minister tell his

listeners that man was basically a terrestrial being and had no business "snooping" around in outer space. He said that other suns and worlds were God's secrets and man shouldn't attempt to meddle in the Creator's private business! He believes that God will stop man from ex-ploring space by direct intervention! In other words, God hasn't stopped man from committing the most atrocious crimes against Universal Law, but now He's going to step in and stop us from taking a closer look at His celestial wonders?

What rubbish! Man is not essentially a terrestrial being . . . he is a spiritual being that takes physical form so that spirit may come to know itself ! How gullible do such ministers think men are? Our ancestors believed that the stars were lights that God set into motion on tracks, and every night sent them around the heavens to amuse His chosen Earth-children! You laugh? And well you might! But the situation is no 'better today. We are told that we must believe that all celestial bodies outside of little Earth are strictly tabu . . . God says: "Hands off!"

This same type of thinking has existed throughout all ages and enslaves mankind. But now the time is at hand, truly our "salvation draweth nigh" . . . man will shortly stand as a true son of God himself ... living in Truth. The vibrations of the New Age will not permit falsity of any kind to exist on Earth. The old falls away . . . all is made new!

Look at present world conditions.. .look at the greatest storms and floods in history . . . look at the wars and rumors of wars . . . look at the strange monsters appearing in the seas and on the mountains of Earth . . . look at the earthquakes in "divers places" . . . and know that "sal-vation is nigh." Yes, there will be chaos on Earth .. . but fear not, for out of the tribulation ahead shall come the most beautiful age man has ever known on Earth, the pitiful little "Red Star."

Do not be deceived by those appointed over you who are in league with Anti-Christ! Believe no one just because lie says it's true . . . do not even believe this book ... listen only to the dictates of your own heart and soul.

"He that shall endure unto the end (of the age), the same shall be saved."

James Russell Lowell said: "Once to every man and nation, comes the moment to decide . . ." Perhaps, also, only once to every planet comes the moment to decide .. . this is, indeed the moment to do just that!

Do not be found asleep . . . watch, for no man know-eth the hour!

Part II — John McCoy

THE GREAT PLAN OF THE SPACE INTELLIGENCES

It is obvious, since we are being visited by -highly in-telligent beings from other planets, that they must have some purpose in their visitation, some intentions toward the inhabitants of Earth. These intentions have been variously assigned and interpreted by individuals on this planet, who in some cases have had contact with the UFOs. Let us begin at the basic possibilities regarding the probable reasons for space visitation at this time.

It is obvious, since we have reports going back many hundreds and even several thousand years, that the space people are not interested in the conquest of the planet by force. Otherwise, we would have certainly been overcome while man was in a primitive state in regard to destructive weapons. Thus we must come to the conclusions that they are passively interested, possibly from a scientific viewpoint, or else that they have the best interests of the people of Earth at heart and are here on a helpful mission. From the many contacts which we believe to be authentic it would seem that the latter is the only logical conclusion. The personal experiences of the authors of this book are sufficient to testify to this, and along with all the other accumulated evidence it is almost a foregone conclusion to the initiate of saucer literature, that the space people are here on a friendly and helpful mission to Earth.

Why should space people suddenly in our time make themselves widely known to mankind by continuous appearance and by contacting comparatively large numbers of Earthlings? Evidently, according to their own messages it is because the planet is nearing the end of a great 26,000 (approximately) year cycle of evolution. The frequency or vibration of Earth is being rapidly raised to a new pitch. It is time that we fulfill our destiny. One came about 2,000 years ago to give man a way of life. He was murdered and his true followers persecuted. When in the time of Constantine, Christianity became very popular, it was decided by those in power, that if men wished to become Christians that they simply would take over the church and permit everyone to have their religion. They would control it and mold it to fit their own ends. Reincarnation was deleted with all its implications—without which concept life becomes a very misunderstood confusion. Thus the religion founded on freedom, love, and devotion became the religion of Constantine the conqueror (who according to some was the incarnation of Judas Iscariot—see SECRET PLACES OF THE LION by G. H. Williamson). Today we find that ministers condone and even encourage their youth to go to war with other nations and kill their fellowman. Some even go so far as to say that "God is on our side!" It is easy to see that the basic principles of the way of life brought 2,000 years ago have been lost and are generally not in practice on Earth.

Now a time has come in the evolution of Earth when man must be ready to enter into a higher consciousness and vibration. Otherwise, he must incarnate elsewhere in order to learn the lessons that will enable him to some-day take his place in the dawning of a New Age on another planet. Those individuals of Earth who are ready to go on, who have learned how to live in peace, love, and harmony with their fellows, will proceed on into a new age, while those who have not will by their own lower rate of vibration eliminate themselves from the picture. As the frequency around us rises, we must also individually improve ourselves in this respect. If we do not, many difficulties are encountered. We are no longer in harmony with our surroundings and we find dissonance. This manifests in many negative conditions and eventually ends in the non-operative condition commonly called death.

Because of the need that humanity has in this coming time, the space people have come here to lend their aid and support. When we hear talk of a new age, we immediately think of everything as being changed and different. All of the bad things of life that annoy ifs, we feel will be eliminated and everything will be so much better. Yes, conditions will be tremendously improved in the new age that approaches. Vast changes will be made, and compared to today it would be called by some a paradise. By Earth standards one supposes that ,it would, indeed, be a paradise. Actually, it is only the way things should be in the first place. People realize this and say that great changes are coming of every conceivable nature. Nothing will be left unchanged. Yet, many forget one thing when they are talking about changes. They know how every-thing is going to change, but many of them forget that they are a part of the old order and that they, too, must change as must the rest! It is very simple to say that everyone will be good and kind and "I'll get along with everyone in the new age." Perhaps we think that there will be no more people in the new age like the next-door neighbor with whom we are not compatible. If we will but look within, we will find that any trouble we are having in the world stems directly from ourselves. Yes, we as individuals must make as many drastic changes within as we will see things changing without. Many of our pet theories and ideas will have to go out the window. Physically, mentally, and spiritually we must adapt to the new order of things.

The spiritual hierarchy of Earth is more or less in charge of the progression of mankind. The hierarchy is composed of the highly-evolved masters and mentors who have reached the state where they have the ability to con-trol matter, energy, space, and time. They recognize to a great extent their own identity and have answered the queston "Who am I?" which gives them great power and ability. They are much concerned with the development of the New Age, of course. Actually, it is evolving under their direction.

Each planet has a counterpart to Earth's hierarchy. None are without their highly advanced teachers and men-tors. On the other planets of this system, the attitudes of the people enable these masters to manifest publicly and so teach, even as did Jesus of Nazareth, Guatama Buddha, and others on this planet. Here it is the exception rather than the rule, however. Because of the fact that Earth has rejected the ancient wisdom so many times and because of the fact that the negative forces are for all purposes and intents in ruling control, it has been necessary for the great teachers to go "underground" to be able to accomplish their missions. The "dark" forces have often attempted in the past to destroy the many manuscripts and documents which contain and preserve the ancient wisdom. Thus even the written word has been secreted through the ages in many places on the face of the Earth. One of these is the Great Pyramid. There are many others. These hidden and secret places are what G. H. Williamson refers to in his book SECRET PLACES OF THE LION. Soon many of these are to be found and the wisdom brought forth for mankind in the new age. Actually, the spiritual hierarchy of earth has been in communication with its counterparts on other planets for millenia and they have worked together at many times.

The spacecraft that are appearing today are under the direction of the hierarchy of their own planets and are working in close harmony with the masters and mystery schools of the hierarchy on Earth. The knowledge of the mystery schools, of the hierarchy, and the master has been brought out by Blavatsky, Alice A. Bailey, Spalding and many others in the past. Today many UFOs are seen in /the areas of the Earth where these schools are located—away from the outer world. Saucers have been seen to land on 'Mt. Shasta where a large center was located until recently. In Tibet they have been seen, and in the jungles of Peru where a number of schools are located.

Thus we see that there is a definite connection between the

mystery schools and the UFO. They are really one and the same force in operation. Just as the FBI has its headquarters in Washington and has many branch offices, so does the spiritual hierarchy have its solar headquar-ters with branches on the planets. When one office has some trouble, help is sent from one of the others so that it can be properly handled. Thus the UFO are in our skies, and we are talking with space men who tell us the same thing that the mentors of this planet have been telling us for many centuries. They operate under the direction of the same force.

Are the space people carrying out their program for the Earth only by contacting certain individuals and hav-ing them write books about the experience and by per-mitting their ships to be seen by many people? No, they are far more active and effective than this. OTHER TONGUES-OTHER FLESH and THEY SHALL BE GATHERED TOGETHER go into great detail in regard to this along with IN SIDE THE SPACE SHIPS and other books in the field. We will not extensively repeat this material, but those of you who do not have a background in what we are about to discuss may desire to know where you may obtain it. As is fairly well known at present, there are many of our brothers from space living among us at the present time. These are individuals which have been landed on the planet from space ships. They have specific tasks and jobs to perform in accordance with the over-all plan and pattern of which many of them are aware to one extent or another. The influence they could have on the society is obvious. New and needed concepts could be easily injected into the cultural stream. Through children's liter-ature, motion pictures, TV, concepts in art, music, morals, religion, and the like, the way of life on this planet could be greatly affected. This is now going on.

Another group doing a very important job are those people referred to as Wanderers by G. H. Williamson in OTHER TONGUES-OTHER FLESH. Briefly, they are individuals from other planets who have volunteered to take up Earth bodies and enter the reincarnational cycle of this planet. (There are a few individuals who have taken over bodies which had previously belonged to entities of the wave of evolution which is peculiar to Earth at the present time. However, most take on Earth bodies at the time of the birth of the body.) These individuals often do not realize their mission 40 Earth, their own true identity, until adulthood. Evidently some even go through full incarnations in Earth bodies without this cognition. Oth-ers remember early in life. In most there are definite signs of identity, this being discussed in full in OTHER TONGUES-OTHER FLESH. The important point here is the part these individuals play in the picture of the purposes of space visitation. Many of them have been contacted by the UFOs for various reasons. They are the space people's "own", so naturally they would be logical contactees —especially those who are aware of their mission and identity.

On June 12, 1956, a very unusual contact was made by the author, Rex and Ray Stanford, Annie Middleton, and David Pillar at the "salt flats" near Brownsville, Texas!. During this contact a crystal device was utilized to direct a beam of energy down upon the group to accomplish certain 'rises and harmonizations of individual frequency rates among members of the groups. Also, certain tests and recordings were evidently made by the space people at that time. The author was able to attain a point of consciousness within the ship and watch the process. When this account was published in THEY SHALL BE GATHERED TOGETHER, some said that such an event was not in harmony with natural law since the space people took a certain initiative in mechanically causing certain changes within each individual present at that contact to enhance their ability and awareness. This was to some a "violation" of the law of Karma. Though these objections are rather vague and beside the point, we might state that the space people observe that an individual is at a certain state of progression and that he is developing quickly toward a specific point at a certain rate. They, with their instrumentation, are able by proper application of high frequency energy, to accelerate the momentum at which the individual is moving toward this specific goal. They accelerate the inevitable.

Rex and Ray Stanford in their book, LOOK UP, describe the sight that they and the author observed on the night of October 21, 1956, shortly after a UFO had passed over-head. Douglas Sharon, the other person present, would involuntarily fall into deep slumber at odd intervals sometimes in the middle of conversation and would be heard to mumble unusual phrases in what seemed to be a foreign tongue, one unknown to the other members of the group. It seems as though the space people were directing certain energies to the young man accelerating his abili-ties and understanding. There were distinct changes and increased awareness evident in Douglas after this contact, all for the better. This has happened in many cases of which we have heard, all over the world. One gentleman, a former yogi, who observed a UFO low over his house, suddenly had the sensation of a tight band being placed around his head and went to bed to sleep for an inordinate amount of time. Several days later he was placed in such a position that he was able to perform a task to help the "cause" of the space people greatly.

Our brothers from space are returning to their own 4nd assisting in their awakening, helping them to remember who they are and what their mission is to Earth. They use many and varied devices to awaken and communicate with those on Earth in whom they are interested.

One common type of communication is a "ringing" in the ears. Evidently the space people while "beaming" down a set of instructions to the subconscious mind of an individual use a device which may cause the sensation of a high-pitched electronic tone signal in the ear. One individual relates that he doubted that the ringing that he often had in his ear was from an extraterrestrial source as he had been told it might be. While he was meditating on this, the ringing began, loud and clear. His first reaction was that he must have an iodine deficiency, which he said often can cause a ringing in the ears. However, within several seconds the ring was modulated into what was evidently some type of code. This continued for several more seconds and the ringing stopped. Unfortunately, the individual did not know Morse code. Needless to say, tnis young man was convinced as to the authenticity of the extraterrestrial origin of his "tone signal" in code. When relating this from the lecture platform, the author has been told by a large number of persons that they have had the same experience. It is quite wide-spread and evidently effective.

More than a few individuals proMinent in the flying saucer fields, who even may appear quite conservative, have had contacts and in some cases are even in fairly constant communication with the UFOs. An individual at the White. Star Illuminator Center at Joshua Tree, California, near Giant Rock, has been able on occasion to "make appointments" for UFO contacts for various people. Many are in communication with the space people on a fairly constant basis. One good example of this was given just a few weeks previous to this writing. Dr. Williamson and the author were on the California desert with a group for the purpose of establishing communications with space people. A gentleman (a channel) in Hollywood told us that he had been informed that we were to have an experience on the desert with the spacecraft. At that time he was not aware that we had been planning to go to the desert for that and other purposes. After a light beam communication set-up had been rigged, we waited for a time with little results. A sensitive in the group, a young man, stated that he kept hearing over and over that we must wait yet a little while. Later that evening he told me quietly to look to the west and that in a short time • would see a large and brilliant blue flare. A few seconds later, the flare did, indeed, appear in the west. It was tremendously large and brilliant. Everyone in the group pf over ten saw it. This is an example of the fact that when the space people desire to have a communication received and there is someone sensitive enough to act as a receiver, then what might be termed paranormal com-munication is an observable phenomenon.

Now the next obvious question is in regard to the nature of the communications that are being received. Just what do they say, and what do they mean to the man in the street. At this moment Dr. Williamson and the au-thor have almost completed an approximately 30,000-mile lecture tour of the United States and Canada. We were able to see some very amazing things while on this trip. From beginning to end we were approached by individ-uals who spoke to us of the various experiments that they and their groups were carrying out. In every conceivable field we found evidence of the hand of the space people. Certainly the new age is not going to simply materialize out of thin air any more than a baby is created totally the instant that it is born. There must be a time of growth and formation when it is not visible in any specific form to the outside world. All over the world the "baby" New Age is in its formative state. After the coming world changes and catastrophe or cataclysm many will look about them and at first see a world shattered and lost, but then suddenly those individuals who have been working under the guidance and instruction of the space people will rise up and say, "Here, look here. We have already begun the development of a new science and way of life." With this the new world will be built and the New Age begun. Already people who are top men in their fields are work-ing on these things. It is only a matter of time until "free energy" principles will be adequately applied. This means devices now requiring electricity will get their energy directly from the "ethers" and will no longer necessitate cords and plugs in the wall. "Television" is now almost perfected with which it is possible to tune in the "other side" with which spiritists are so concerned. Whole new concepts in science, religion, and the arts are being applied. Scientology, New Age psychology, now makes it possible for people to tremendously increase their abili-ties and intelligence, something never before accomplished to this extent. If it were possible to state just who the individuals are who are working on these devices, the reader might be very surprised. Top names are involved, some of which all would know. The greatest work is being done by those individuals who are working quietly and unobtrusively. They are not the persons writing books in most cases or anyone who is-in the public eye. The important people are the scientists, for example, who go up to the mother ships once a week to work in the laboratories there or to attend discourses, The people who sit down at a drawing board and begin to receive plans for various instruments or scenes, of other planets, those who are writing the new music, those who are performing the IQ-raising experiments in psychology, are the ones who are doing an important work. The New Age is developing well, but it has yet to be born. At the proper time it will be ready.

The most amazing thing that was observed cross-country was this: In every little town and city, almost, we encountered people working along the same lines, even though they had never heard of each other and in some cases knew almost nothing about UFOs. Everywhere there was talk of crystals, piezo effects, copper pyramids and cones, etc., etc. To us this was the greatest proof that could be offered as to the validity of the messages that have come from the various contacts. This showed us that a master plan was in operation, being worked out from a central point. All over the Earth a great army is rising up. It is an army whose conquests are in the fields of knowledge—that man might live, rather than die. When you come across two, three, four and then more and more people who are working on developing the same thing or something of a complimentary nature, then you see that the guidance of the space people and the spiritual hierarchy of this planet are things which are very real and very active.

The evidence is startling and amazing. Science fiction has not even begun to conceive the drama that is being enacted on our planet. Fantasy writers might laugh at the story saying that it was too unrealistic! Yet, it is true! A mighty force is being built which will build a world. When the New Age is nigh, and the people ask, "Now what shall we do? Return to the caves?", the answer will come from those who have developed already the new way of life. They will bring forth their knowledge and develop-ments and teach these things to those who are left. Thus the teachers of the remnant that will remain are flow be-ing prepared as are the subjects which are to be taught. Some ask, "Where is this New Age?" Open your closed eyes, ears, and hearts. Look about you. Lo, the great Earth makes ready to bring forth a child.

THE DRAMA OF EARTH'S GREAT DELUSION

In the first half of this book Earth is spoken of as the "prison world". One might also term it the great lunatic asylum! Perhaps some will take this statement wrongly as unfair criticism or judgment of the people of this planet. It is not that the people were psychotic and placed in this asylum so much as it is that the conditions of the planet enforce and propagate the insanity. Of course, we are not on what has been termed by some as "trash can No. 7" for nothing. There are reasons. In reality, how-ever, our plight is not so bad for we are "envied" by many people living on highly advanced planets. To some this is inconceivable. The facts of the matter are this: As we put strain on a muscle — as we use it over and over again to overcome the power of gravity in lifting a mass—we build that muscle. As we bring into play our spiritual and other "muscles" to overcome the tremendous nega-tivity around us everyday, we become correspondingly more and more powerful and developed from this view-point. Man on earth has a tremendous opportunity if he will but take advantage of it. Particularly in modern times as we near the end of the age, does man have this opportunity. All things are extremely speeded-up and we may make in a single day, perhaps, the progression that might have required months or even years at a less opportune time. Therefore, we are guilty of great negligence when we permit ourselves to lag behind and not do as much as we can to enable ourselves and others to take ad-vantage of this present condition.

We have said that the Earth is an asylum. Truly many people have been overcome by the negative conditions that reign here and have lost awareness of reality. Perhaps this could be the best definition of any type of insanity. It is merely the loss of ability to view a thing or things or all things with any degree of accuracy. When this hap-pens, an individual loses agreement with his fellow man and he is placed apart from society. Now what happens if all society loses its sense of balance, its ability to view things as they really are? It is obvious that those few who remain who are able to be aware of basic reality will be outcasts of society if they try to express their views to those who are deluded.

If you wanted to absolutely control a world, how would you go about it? Obviously, the best type of control is hidden control. If the people were convinced that they were free, that they controlled themselves, that others on the other side of the planet were enslaved by dictators, they would never give any thought to the person or per sons who pulled the puppet strings. If a country were thoroughly convinced if its "freedom" and that it had to protect this "freedom" from "aliens", then we could find the great insanity of war—men killing their brothers. We find, then, the problem of control being not so much the necessity of having great power and many men to do your bidding, but convincing all that you are not in control—that they are free to make their own choices— but then be-hind the scenes, controlling them completely! How fantastic. How could this possibly be accomplished? First it is necessary not only to have the smoke screen of people thinking that they are free, but also we must focus their attention on something which they will think is a real danger or threat to them. If we can convince them that they must be very careful and watchful of a certain group in a part of the world remote from them, then all their attention and fear will 'be directedtoward this group and never toward the real controlling power. This also makes wars possible and wars are a very important part of our scheme of world slavery. If we are to present the illusion of freedom, we cannot make the people do things that they do not want to do! Our problem is to control the people's desires. Economics are the method we shall use for our system of control. If we develop an advanced technology with all sorts of work-saving devices which sell for large amounts of money, and if we create a desire for a great many of these products, we find that people are willing to sell themselves to others in order to gain sufficient money to purchase these objects. This is an economic slavery. A person, for example, wants to buy a TV set. In addition to the cost of a TV set the individual has continuous living expenses of food, shelter, and clothing. It is possible for the individual to purchase the TV set on time payment plans. In other words one does not have to have cash in hand to pay for an item if he is willing to pay a little more for use of the device until he pays for it completely. Therefore, we get this picture. A man goes out to work all day in order to earn enough money to eat and have shelter and clothing so that he can go out and work and have enough money to eat and have shelter and clothing. Then he is told that he must buy a TV set, a refrigerator, a new car, a washing machine, etc., ad infinitum. Thus he works harder and harder to meet these payments on these various mechanical devices which entertain (?) and save labor. (He labors harder to purchase devices which save labor—it doesn't quite make sense.) TV is an excellent method for us to use to indoctrinate our captives. They are kept busy all day at the office or the factory so that they can come home and enjoy the luxury of watching TV for a few hours. On TV we see to it that they are bombarded with more orders to buy this or that and that also on most of the shows, materialistic prop-aganda is propagated openly and with subliminal projections.

The whole crux of our plan is seeing to it that the public becomes innured with basic materialistic, ideas. It is through their desire for material luxury that we control them. People go to college in many cases so that they can make more money. This money will buy them the things they want. They in any case must spend most of their time and energy in pursuing and taking care of this money. Their main intentions in life are directed towards the goal of making enough money to have the things they want to have. We determine what they want to have by telling them over and over what it is they want and by making the more general desires simply accepted by everyone so that little children grow up with these opinions. By placing an enemy on the horizon who will, we will tell them, enslave them if they get a chance, who will take away their TV sets and jobs and so forth, we place any attention that might remain after chasing the dollar all day and watching TV all evening, on this threat.

Freedom basically means being able to do what you want to do when you want to do it. We do not mean here an Aladdin's Lamp must be given to everyone, but merely that one should be able to in a reasonable amount of time accomplish the things which he desires to do. Most people say, "If I didn't have a job to keep and a family to support, I'd do such and such." The controllers of humanity have set up a great materialistic doctrine by which men are to govern their lives. They have also set up a great ,economic system which most are forced to enter and to which they must confine themselves. Those who do not are considered to be to one degree or another insane and are generally outcast from any position in the society. The person who controls the money of the world controls the people. By creating demands and supplies, by creating enough problems for everyone to worry about, he insures first continued control by money and secondly continued security for one's own position by a cloud of secrecy. How can one, after all, be deposed if no one realizes you are there to be deposed? The goal is to keep people fairly com-fortable but to keep their time occupied with mundane things and inhibit their individuality and awareness. Set up governments and various agencies which think for them. Let a certain agency pronounce that a thing is thus and so and if enough prestige and "officialness" is given to the organization, their statement will be accepted no matter how absurd or foolish it may be. For example, people consume deadly poisons in their food each day of the cumulative variety (a poison which is cumulative will build up in deposits in the body until it eventually will cause death of the individual in one way or another; per-haps deposits such as arthritic conditions, gallstone, etc., are a result of consumption of poisons which are of the cumulative variety.) Yet, when the average person is told this he responds by saying, "If that were true our pure food and drug people would not allow it to be sold to us!" It is inconceivable to him that it is possible that the agency he refers to is unreliable. He refuses to look at the chemical facts of the situation. His trust is with vested authority. ft has been indelibly traced in his mind that these things (governments, agencies, etc.) are infallible. He can believe nothing' else.

There is one other little point to be brought out here. When war becomes expedient to boost a failing economy 'and to get rid of excess population, etc., then it is simple to arrange an incident which will cause one. War is a handy little tool. First' one must lay the groundwork of materialistic concepts and desires, and then we work from there. When man learns to love unselfishly, he will no longer be able to kill another of his fellow creatures. But as long as hate can be instilled in his heart, the beast can control his thoughts and will.

Give thought to the foregoing paragraphs. Could this have happened on our planet? What do you think? The answer should be rather clear, at least to those who can still think.

When we have close contact with the space people we will find that the materialism and negative concepts which have been cultivated on Earth will show up greatly. We will find their ideas to be very much different than those of Earth. They actually have no economy as such and their ideas on the basic factors of social living are vastly different. Many Earthlings would be shocked and sur-prised to know of some of the ideas of the space people. They would be considered odd, indeed. Man must gradually come out of the many negative concepts with which he has grown up. As we said, each individual must rid himself of the old if he is to enter into the new. On Earth most things which look black are white and those which look white are black. (This is from the standpoint of the average man.) When we get to a certain point in our Search for truth, we suddenly find that we are no longer able to converse with many people on a level that they understand. We find that we have gotten to the point that we cannot say everything we think to everyone or they would believe we were mad! With some it is only possible to discuss the weather without coming acrorss points which would bring violent differences of opinion if we expressed our views. (Even the weather can be a touchy subject.) This is an asylum, all right, but as we become more and more aware and more and more sane, we bcome the ones who are considered insane!

Perhaps psychology is one of the greatest examples that we might give of the propagation of the materialistic, atheistic, communistic, doctrine that is so enslaving. To begin with psychology means a study of the soul. How-ever, no one operates on this basis in the "science". In leading texts we find that psychology must be defined in terms of its "history". Actually we find that the existence of a soul is debunked in psychology and man is simply considered a machine operating as the effect of outside stimuli. Perhaps some would like to reduce us to that state, but this is not the true nature of man.

On Earth a great drama is being acted out. One force hopes to hold its control over man, the other hopes to liberate him. It is up to each man to choose his way. "Either you are with me or you are against me." There is no half-way point. Men would not believe the truth if it were presented to them. It is too fantastic.

As more and more of this information comes to light, and more and more people are aware of it, the leaders in the New Age fields may undergo serious trials. If they become dangerous to those who would keep man a beast, the hidden rulers may take action against them. In times past this has happened when someone has said too much to too many people. At present the authors in the flying saucer field are still considered lunatics, liars, etc. by most people, so they pose no threat to the powers that be. As soon as they do, however, we will see proof of some of the things herein stated! Perhaps the 13th Chapter of Mark, as mentioned in THEY SHALL BE GATHERED TOGETHER, has some bearing on this situation. "And when ye shall hear of wars and rumors of wars, be ye not troubled: for such things must needs be; but the end shall not be yet. For nation shall rise against nation and kingdom against kingdom : and there shall be earthquakes in divers places, and there shall be famines and troubles: these are the beginnings of sorrows. But take heed to yourselves : for they shall deliver you up to councils; and in the synagogues ye shall be beaten : and ye shall be brought before rulers and kings for my sake, for a testimony against them. And the gospel must first be published among all nations. But when they shall lead you, and deliver you up, take no thought beforehand what ye shall speak, neither do ye premeditate: but whatsoever shall be given you in that hour, that speak ye : for it is not ye that speak but the Holy Ghost." For they shall deliver you up. ... . These are the words of prophecy. We can see why certain people would be delivered up in view of the true facts about this planet. But we also have the promise, "but he that shall endure unto the end, the same shall be saved."

As these new things begin to work out, be not surprised at the very unusual ideas and opinions which are brought to light. Changes of a revolutionary nature are going to be made in our concepts from diet to economy! Let's wake up and look around us and find out what is going on and seek some new ideas and understanding of life.

The drama is a fantastic one, but it becomes even more fantastic in a moment. Two forces are vieing for life on this planet—one that makes men slaves and one that makes men free. Yet, there is a third force which evidently is detached from the other two, at least to the extent that it would aid one simply because it was against the other. It has a bearing on many of the seeming contradictions in some of the more controversial contact stories. In our next phase of questioning we will take a look at the things which are in space ships which might not have such good intentions toward our planet as our Venusian and other friends from this solar system!

THE GREAT ENIGMA

Perhaps the greatest enigma in flying saucer research is the seeming contradictions among the stories of the various saucer contactees. This is always an excellent point for an individual with the "will not to believe" to bring up in debating the saucer subject. We all are aware enough of the fact that when a story is passed from one person to another, many changes of both a minor and oc-casionally a major nature are bound to occur. Also it would be impossible to perfectly duplicate everything one saw aboard a spaceship or for that matter in a modern factory. To interpret correctly what we saw would be an even more difficult task. Probably the following story (fictional) is the best example of the reasons for many of the seeming contradictions. It seems a space ship came to Earth and the captain sent three men out separately to its surface to investigate it. When they reported back this is what they said. The first reported that it was extremely cold on the Earth, that everyone wore heavy furs, ate whale blubber and lived in ice houses. He had landed in northern Alaska. The second said that it was a very hot and tropical place with a good deal of moisture. All the natives went about almost naked, were black and killed a variety of wild animals for food. Their houses were of grass. This fellow had landed in Africa. The third space-man landed in New York! You can well imagine that his description of what he saw was sufficient to cause even more confusion than the reports of his two fellow "reporters". Thus we see perhaps a little more lucidly just why some reports may be a little contradictory and diversified. Indeed, if they were not, then this would be the time to cry "Hoax!"

However, there are some things which have been said to have come from the space people which are in direct violation of some of the things which are more or less definitely agreed upon by all. One of these is in regard to atomic energy. This is a destructive force and the people of this solar system do not use it according to many sources which have in the past fairly well authenticated themselves. This one particular point is so readily demonstrable that in the past many have used it for a criterion in judging other saucer stories. When several appeared in which the space people allegedly urged the "peaceful use of atomic energy" those who were "in the know" in saucer research were forced to reject these stories as atomic energy in the sense of fusion and fission simply is not in use elsewhere in this solar system. (For details on this see OTHER TONGUES-OTHER FLESH by Wil-liamson.)

The great enigma developed when it was discovered that some of the individuals who had claimed contact and who had made statements of such a contradictory nature as to definitely brand themselves with the taint of prevarication were found to have had at least some of the experiences they claimed! They had made statements which were very, very doubtful in the light of experiences which the author and good friends of the author personally knew to be true, yet from irrefutable sources the information was relayed that those persons had had some some very unusual experiences evidently with space people. This is the great enigma which has been developing in the saucer field in the past few months in particular.

A prime example can be given here without mention-ing any names. A certain person claimed contact with the UFOs by various means. Many witnesses saw on at least one occasion, a tremendous ship arrive over a large city at the request of this individual via the methods of communication being used that night. Things occurred which could not be laid entirely to coincidence. Yet, at a later date this same person was caught in extremely dishonest acts and hoaxes of no uncertain nature. Why would space people seemingly cooperate with such unscrupulous characters? Evidently this has happened in several cases. What is the reason? Another common de-nominator to these unusual cases seems to be exaggeration on the part of the "contactee" of the original incident so as to enhance the story. There is something basically wrong here. What is it?

Is it possible that all of space may not be "good" or working for the betterment of man? Some seem to have the rather naive idea that anything from outer space is all "love and light". Evidently we have more than one force visiting our planet according to space intelligences. To understand what is going on we may look back many millenia in the past history. Thousands of years ago, it is said, there existed what was known as the Galactic Administration. It was an organization which included thousands of worlds in our Milky Way Galaxy. The Administration was governed by a tremendous "electronic brain" or mechanical computer which evidently covered the entire surface on one small planet. Eventually it was found that rule by machine brought about degeneration and a type of revolution took place. A gentleman by the name of Elron was evidently one of the top figures in this revolt. His, and the efforts of many others, resulted in the dissolution of the Administration (and not too peacably either, in some areas). Out of the remains of this came two forces. One was mainly a group of space pirates whose headquarters centered and still center in the Orion Nebula. The other group continued to use the electronic brain to some degree in matters of science and for other minor purposes and attempted to rebuild the administration on more workable lines. The pirates tended to prey on the more peaceful planets, which formed what was called the Space Confederation. The Orionites were quite materialistic and destructive.

Evidently the evolved ancestors of the pirates of Orion and the Space Confederation are visiting Earth at the present time. The Orionites may be classed as the destructive force while the Space Confederation is attempting to help their brothers on this planet to fulfill their destiny. The pirates would like very much to tow Earth out of its orbit and even out of the solar system and to utilize its mineral resources. Annihilation of the entire population would be necessary to accomplish that end.

At the present time we are told the Space Confederation is holding the planet against the Orion forces to permit Earth to work out its destiny without great interference such as annihilation of all life in a few moments. Nevertheless, the Orionites have evidently been working to bring about confusion and negativity in the New Age movement with an eye to the failure of the plans of the Space Confederation. It is possible and perhaps even probable that some individuals have been contacted by negative space people who hope to spread confusion and dissention by giving enough information of a loving and brotherly nature which agrees with Space Confederation contacts and then put in a few pertinent bits of data which conflict with the way things really are. It is easy to say "I am a Venusian" when you are really from Orion. The main question we have to ask is not in regard to the reality of the contact but as to what was contacted. It is firmly believed that not more than a very few out and out hoaxes have occurred in this field, but the probability is strong that more than one have been contacted by those desiring to bring about the destruction of man. Even the "elect" may be deceived by those of a negative nature at first glance. However, we must not only recognize the negative forces in outer space but on our own planet. As ever, they are quite able to deceive even the best intentioned of people. Forces from the so-called astral plane and other levels of discarnate life are able to contact the realm of the "living" often with intentions which are not entirely benevolent. A discarnate can impersonate a Venusian as easily as anyone else, if not easier. Also some seem to think that simply because an entity is free of the "bondage" of the physical body, that it is possessed of all truth and knowledge, when in actuality they know no more than when they were "living" in many cases. We would not talk to Grandma when she was alive, but when she is dead, her words are at a premium!

Let us not construe this to mean that it is not possi-ble to receive messages and impressions from the space people or the spiritual hierarchy via extra-sensory perception or reputable channels of information. We should, however, take this out of the realm of "phenomena" and look upon it in its true light, simply a means of commu-nication. Yet many will claim that there are inaccuracies in all the messages received in such a way, and doubtlessly they are correct in this claim. With negatives pos-ing as Venusians and the like, "astrals" being thrilled by the importance attached to their words by a naive audience, and inaccuracies in the best of channels, how do we know what is what? We are told that there will be many false prophets and many will be fooled. But in the same breath we are also told how to determine the false. The little saying "By their fruits shall ye know them" is our key. Perhaps we have overlooked it in the past due to its extreme simplicity. Nevertheless, it is the key that was given. If a teaching is constructive in its intent and content, if it points the individual to the "god within" and not to the teacher, if it says to seek for more wisdom and not that herein is contained all wisdom or even great wisdom that cannot be found elsewhere, then examine what it says. If from the words you find concepts which you can use for your and others' benefit, then use the information. If you are not able to use it, leave it alone. However, always refrain from condemning anything simply because you cannot understand or use it. Everything has some meas-ure of truth if we can but find it. Thus be selective and look to the fruits of the material in order to discover the best and the most effective information.

In regard to the contacting of negatives we find some very excellent information in the January-February, 1958, issue of the WHITE STAR ILLUMINATOR. (This is a very excellent publication which is recommended quite highly as its

material is unique and as the title implies, most illum-
inating. It is distributed on a contribution basis and may be
obtained from White Star Illuminator, P. o. Box 307, Joshua
Tree, California.) This paragraph is from an ar-ticle entitled
"Ships and Their Purpose".

"You are instructed to use *caution* in any and all contacts, for
not all are of *positive constructive intent.* NEGATIVES from
outer-space are no longer capable of penetrating our filter-
screen. However, the *negatives* of your world are rampant.
This includes the Astral-Band. Love is the KEY by which they
can be detected. No master of darkness can project LOVE
frequency. It would manifest as sex-stimulation. Do not let
this thought alarm you. Sex impulses of a *lustful* nature are
quite discernable from sex-impulses of a DIVINE NATURE.
Think this one over! The heart is the KEY here. *Sex force is
Light* when properly understood and utilized. The Universes
of God are based on *Polarity.* This will be a topic of
discussion at a later date. Much has been written on this
subject inspired by the MASTERS OF LIGHT for the *earnest
seeker of truth."*

Negativity is discernable quite readily if we will but judge the
amount of survival any action will give to the greatest
number of people and things. If it will decrease survival more
than it will increase it, then the action is destructive or
negative. Let us be not quite so ready to "go overboard" on
anything we hear or read. Let us keep our feet on the ground
and use the sure scientific method given to us by the master
of Galilee. "By their fruits shall ye know them". Take a look
and see just what the fruits really are.

TO SEDUCE EVEN THE ELECT

We have shown how the negative forces are in control of the entire Earth. It is probably obvious to most of you by now. However, some will think it is meant that there is a vast network of underlings and a vast communications system through which many receive their orders. Some will place the so-called newspaper censorship of flying saucers at the door of the internationalists. They may think that each editor of a large newspaper receives his daily "orders" from the offices of top conspirators. Nothing could be farther from the truth. Those controlling the world have their only safety in making the people think that they are self-controlled. Never would they be so public as to threaten large numbers of individuals. They are responsible for the suppression of flying saucer information from all sources, nevertheless. They are directly keeping the governmental channels devoid of any admissions of the interplanetary nature of the UFO. And they are responsible for closing the public's mind to the existence of the extraterrestrial visitors also. Yet, they do not issue orders to editors and other individuals of a similar status. They covertly close the mass mind by cleverly inducing the dialectic materialism of Marx and Wundt, and of communist Russia—the belief that man is but mud and we should eat, drink and be merry because one of these tomorrows we may die. They subtly, over the years, beginning in childhood, initiate the individual into the concepts which are necessary for him to be enslaved.

The first and primary concept which must be im-planted in the mind of youth is the idea of the mass mind. He must learn that the "majority" does indeed rule; that the person who goes against the "mob" must endure the pain of ostracism from what makes up the society today. The path of an intelligent and individualistic person is a lonely path, indeed. The youth is pounded with the idea that he must be a part of the social group, going to dances, drinking cokes, striving to make the honor role, dress like the gang, and in general, conform to the mass mold. Young men, at least in many areas of the United States, are laughed at and made fun of by their more conforming fellows for the simple offense of wearing dress slacks and not the customary "blue jean". This one deviation from the norm (so-called) can result in the complete rejection of an individual by teenage groups in the U. S. today.

One of the quickest means the negative forces have for indoctrinating youth into the ways of the "mass mind" are the so-called physical education classes in public schools. The foul seeds of regimentation which are planted in the individuals during everyday life are brought to full fruition in the atmosphere created in these classes. Here full regimentation is required in most cases and all creative urges stifled. The most savage and brutal animalistic instincts are brought out in impressionistic and pliable youth as they are placed, often deliberately, in circumstances which would be unbearable to a delicate and creative personality. of any intellectual standards. Because of this and the other conditions encountered in schools and social life, the individual must compeltely conform or suffer the consequences, which in cases of those- with high intellectual capacities can prove highly deleterious. The author has personally witnessed the progressive personality disintegration of students with near genius I.Q.'s as they went year by year through American school systems, until a condition of neurosis had set in. In other extremely intelligent individuals an attitude of apathy resulted. It was impossible to effectively rebel against the accepted codes and mass standards, so they simply succumbed to regimentation and became a part of the "pattern" losing the individual creativity, merely retaining sufficient ability to make a comfortable living. They outwardly were like all the other "normal" people, but inwardly there remained a spark of creative imaginative force which urged them to venture forth and dare to be different. But this was suppressed! They dare not express it for they know the consequences of being different in a mob obsessed with the idea that everyone must be identical in mind and action.

Perhaps you think it is harsh to lay the blame for much of this deplorable situation at the doorstep of the schools and in particular of the physical education classes. My evidence is not only from firsthand observation in a number of institutions of "education" (or would a better term be "brainwashing") and interviews with a large number of students from all over the U. S., but from the following. A short time ago I was on a weekly radio panel which discussed subjects of timely interest. There had been some adverse publicity regarding the physical education classes in the local schools and our group had invited the co-ordinator for these classes for the entire city to discuss this topic with us. During a warm-up session held the afternoon before the broadcast (which did grow quite "hot") the public official made it clear that he would not be on the program if there was to be any criticism of the classes and the methods used in them. He self-righteously declared that according to his superiors at a state level, the purpose of physical education classes was to bring as much conformity and regimentation as possible into each boy participating (and it is law that all must participate). "They must be brought to the point where they will accept the orders or ideas of their instructors without question, without thinking. This is to prepare them for war where they must act as unquestioning machines in response to the orders given. The youth of the country must be developed into a killing and destructive force so that our country, our women and children, can be protected from the devils that would invade our free land!" The idea that anyone should question what seemed to this gentleman high ideals and necessary measures for protecting the United States from foreign "dogs", seemed completely unreasonable and un-American. He did not stop to think that his own ideas were ungodly! If you do not believe these words, spend a week or two in a school visiting all classes and observe the restrictions and conformity which are rampant. Creative thinking and imagination are tabu in American youth today.

Crime and degeneracy are prime characteristics of the present generation. It is necessarily so if we are to breed a generation that will carry on the inhuman cruelty of war and greed and lust which are the common denominators of our culture. The straight and clear-thinking minds of youth must be warped and twisted into patterns of hate and lust if power is to be retained by those who have grown fat on the bodies of young men, children and women, all innocent of any crime save being born on Earth and being susceptible to the malevolent influence of the reigning culture. It is said that Hitler stated that if he could gain control of the educational system of a country but for a few years, he would control that country. Do not think that this important rule of control has been over-looked by the powers that be! Anyone naive enough to think that the schools of America are not polluted and saturated with the vicious and insidious specter of the godless monsters who feed upon their own kind, are in for a shock when and if they ever investigate!

Youth is forced into the mass mind or they are forced to an ineffective insanity! We learn we must conform, have respect for authority and act upon what authority says. If the internationalists are in control of all author-ity, they are in effect in control of the world. They mold mass opinion and beliefs and thus are far more effective than if they had the forces to occupy the world from a military standpoint. They control thinking and action, not just action. For example, students of modern psy-chology are taught that esoteric studies are "mind-med-dling". They are also taught that when they discover some inability or abberation in themselves that the best course is to "adjust" or simply learn to live with it. How much more apathetic can a philosophy become?

To see the able minds of youthful men and women twisted by insidious propaganda from schools, TV, music, cheap literature, movies, and from practically every other source of information which they contact, is heart-rending. To know the potential that man of earth possesses and to see the noble thoughts which are natural to man trampled in the dust beneath the hooves of the thundering herd, which no longer resembles humankind in any way except form, makes one understand the sorrows of Jesus as he looked out upon this deluded world. Not only are we a part of the greatest drama, but also the greatest tragedy of all time.

Why all the juvenile delinquency? A goodly portion of crimes by youth are performed by those of the higher intelligence brackets. One particular case of which the author has personal knowledge is especially interesting from this viewpoint. The young man involved had an I.Q. of 158 according to school tests. This would place him in the upper one percent of the entire nation. Yet, he conformed completely to accepted standards (and ac-cepted standards to the higher toned and more intelligent are more often than not, criminal in nature!) and was a very difficult discipline problem. He was capable of intelligent conversation and could at will perform perfectly any scholastic task given him. Yet, most of the time his behaviour was that of a ten or eleven-year-old child of bad temperament. He was rebelling against a hostile society which forced him to be what he was if he was to gain any acceptance from the "average" teenager! The public would be shocked to know the extent of criminal acts among the youth of the nation and the fact that the "well-bred" sons and daughters of well-to-do people are seriously involved in these activities in many, many cases. Genius and creative ability have been lost in the morass of conformity and amalgamation into the mass mind of materialism.

How can we expect much information on the UFOs and their message to penetrate the public mind when it has been filled from childhood with such a tremendous block to rational thinking. Look about you and see how many people are really sane and aware of things which are going on around them. How many are "hypnotized" or fixated on the trivia that make no difference in the long run? How many of them give any thought as to why they are on Earth or what purpose there is to life? How many are really living and how many are simply the "vertical dead"? Look around you and shudder! New' Age information is effectively blocked from penetration into the mass mind of man. Our only access is with the individ-ual and then it is often very difficult.

Even in the UFO field itself, we find many people fixating on the little details. Because of the personality or personal life of a contactee, for example, some people feel his story can not be true. They ignore the teaching and look for faults in the teacher. They look to trivia which ,make no difference in the long run. They ask if the ex-perience was physical or astral or etheric. They are con-cerned with the color and direction in which the UFO moved. They are concerned with everything except the important thing. There is a New Age dawning on the planet. Whether space people are here or not makes no difference. Whether the contactees are telling the truth or not makes no difference. Look to yourself and discover your own shortcomings and take what you can from the teachings around you to make up for and fill these deficits. When the student has prepared himself to use and accept information, it will be brought to him. This is an immutable law. Prepare yourself, look around you, and then know what is going on around you. You do not have to believe anyone, simply prepare yourself and you will know for yourself. Let us not fall victim to the fallacy of looking at the tiny details and never getting far enough from the picture to see what it is all about.

Earth is controlled by a great negative force. This force is about to bring on its own destruction. Earth is about to graduate into a new era of understanding for the "remnant" that remains. Visitors are coming across space to help their brothers of Earth to enter this new era. There will be many difficulties to surmount and many burdens to bear by all who wish to become a part of the new for they must be purged of the old and brought into a quick realization of that now dawning. We live in a world ruled by hate and fear, not love and understanding. If there are a few who have some understanding, it is criminal for them not to attempt to increase their own ability and to help their fellow man to achieve the same. Those of you who work for the evolution of man in love and understanding , forget your differences and band together in love and peace to learn to live so that many may be awakened and enter into the new.

The UFOs have turned the spotlight on the sores of Earth that at least some might be saved and healed of their delusions . There are those who would block the lights and keep these things secret, but they will not succeed for light is always brought to those who ask for it. The Night is over and the Day is dawning ! It is the day for which so many have worked so long. Awaken to its healing rays and look sanely about and begin to clean up the vile mess which confronts you! Look, Know and then Act in love and peace so that you and your fellows might live once more as man should live ! Let the Plan be restored on Earth !

www.ingramcontent.com/pod-product-compliance
Lightning Source LLC
Chambersburg PA
CBHW051146020726
47501CB00005B/1702